JORDAN'S BRAINS

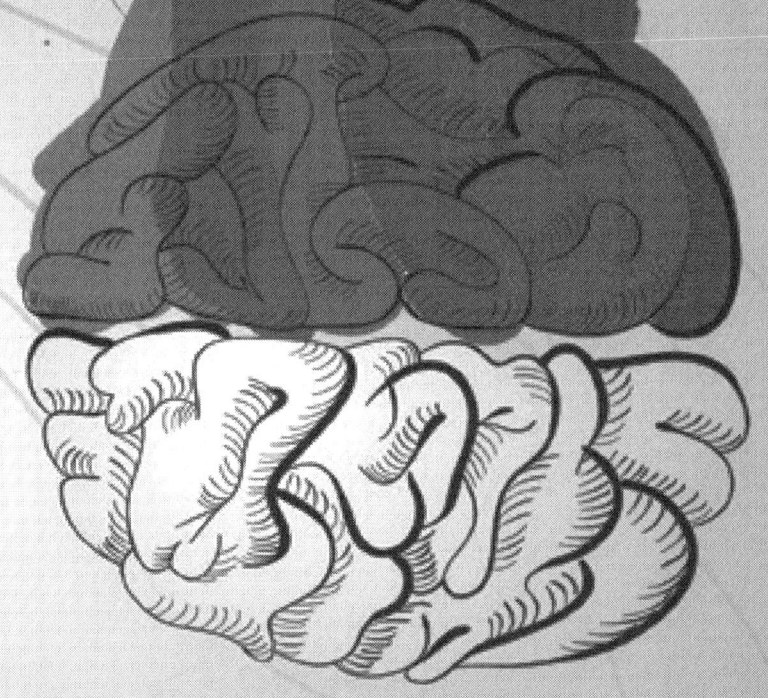

XXXXXXXXXXXXXXXXXXXXXXX
XX A ZOMBIE EVOLUTION XX
XXXXXXXXXXXXXXXXXXXXXXX

J. CORNELL MICHEL
XXX

Copyright © 2013 J. Cornell Michel
All rights reserved.
ISBN: 1482313502
ISBN 13: 9781482313505
Library of Congress Control Number: 2013902214
CreateSpace Independent Publishing Platform
North Charleston, South Carolina

For Kenric

Anne,

   Thank you for reading my book. I hope you enjoy it! Zombies are people too :)

   -Jillian

CHAPTER 1

I have always known the greatest period of my life would be a dark time for the rest of the world. That time has finally come, and I can't say that I'm not excited to meet my first zombie. I'm not your average zombie expert. I live in a tiny room on the third floor of a psychiatric hospital. I'm not a psychopath; my brain just works a little differently than that of the average person.

I live in the voluntarily committed wing at Gardner House, a three-story brick building that was built in the 1970s. Everyone knows it's a mental hospital, but they call it *Gardner House* because it sounds better. I'd rather not live in this place, but my mom pays for me to stay here, because she thinks I'm unstable. I don't need constant supervision, and I can leave Gardner House if I give twenty-four hours' notice. I even have a part-time job. My doctor thinks it will help me have a more normal life. Well, being normal doesn't matter anymore. Zombies don't discriminate; they'll eat any brain they can sink their infected teeth into. I'm sure my unique brain tastes the same as a normal brain. Actually, mine might be slightly tastier.

I turn up the volume on my tiny television so I can hear the latest coverage of the zombie invasion. They just confirmed this morning that there is a highly contagious disease spreading throughout the country. Symptoms of this horrific illness include fever, death, resurrection, and finally (naturally) cannibalism. That can only mean one thing: the zombies are finally here.

I start preparing to leave the safety of my room to venture out into the zombie-infested streets. I pull on my favorite pair of worn jeans and slip on my most comfortable sneakers. Everyone should be comfy during the apocalypse. I pull on a black T-shirt with the words "Zombie Slayer" written on the front in white letters. I cover my short, black hair with a Brooklyn Dodgers cap. I don't really pay attention to sports, but I have a collection of hats for sports teams that no longer exist. I like to pay my respects to displaced teams.

I peer out my tiny window and check the street for zombies. I see a figure across the street, aimlessly roaming around the park, but I can't tell if it's a human or a zombie. I notice the sun glinting off the lake across the street, and there isn't a cloud in the afternoon sky. I never thought the zombies would start their invasion on such a lovely day. Speaking of lovely, I try to call my mom one more time, but there's no answer. This is the third time I have called, and I can't stand the thought of her being on her own during the zombie apocalypse.

I study zombies every day, so I know exactly what to do. More importantly, I know what *not* to do. I refuse to be among those idiots who crash their cars into nearby trees in the first five minutes of the movie. I have seen every zombie movie ever released, as well as most other horror movies, and some are created purely for entertainment, while others are educational. For example, *Zombieland* is one of my favorite movies, and it offers plenty of good advice on how to stay alive during a zombie invasion. *Army of Darkness*, while not technically a zombie movie, is entertaining, but it doesn't really teach you anything useful (unless you need to know if something is a trick and whether or not to get an axe).

For the past few years, I have been working on a zombie fact booklet. Please do not confuse this with a survival guide: my booklet is not about survival; it's about knowledge. The more you know about zombies, the more likely you'll be able to live through their rampage. My booklet includes zombie facts, as well as ways to help people who are in trouble.

I grab a stack of booklets, my collection of East Coast maps, and my bug-out bag. I quietly open the door to my room, careful not to make a sound. I head to the stairs at the end of the hall, knowing better than to take the elevator. Almost certainly, the elevator doors will open to reveal a swarm of zombies. The stairs are usually a safe bet. I creep along the abandoned hallway, slowly making my way to the stairs. Sun pours through the large hallway windows and reflects off the blindingly white walls and scuffed, white linoleum. The smell of antiseptic is in the air, and it reminds me that I should be grateful for the way things are now, because this place won't be as pretty after we're a few months into the zombie apocalypse. My mind flashes to the carnage in the zombie movie I was watching just last night: blood pooling near the heads of fresh corpses, guts spilled on the ground, and, of course, brains all over the place (lots and lots of brains).

I try to shake the disturbing images from my mind so I can focus on my plan. The main characters in zombie movies usually try to save their families first. In *Shaun of the Dead*, Shaun saved his mom before saving his girlfriend, which is a choice I fully support. I don't have a significant other, because I've never really had time for romantic relationships. I have much more important things to worry about, like saving the world from zombies.

Anyway, back to the plan: first, save your family, and then save the world. But it's also OK to help other people while you're on your way to saving your family. One thing I've never liked about zombie movies is the way the characters act toward strangers; it's always everyone for himself. Or herself. You shouldn't leave people to die just because you don't know them. Even though saving your family should be your main goal, you should try to help as many people as possible, because it's the right thing to do.

My brother and sister both live nearby. We all grew up in Maryland, and we decided to stay in the area. It's not that we love it here; we're just too lazy to move away. I'm comfortable at Gardner House, and my siblings like to be nearby to keep an eye on me. My mom lived in Maryland her whole life, but she moved to Jacksonville, Florida five months ago, which is terribly inconvenient for me. The day she moved to Florida, I mapped out a rescue route so I would be ready to drive down and pick her up at a moment's notice.

I snap back to reality when I hear a crash come from the opposite end of the hall. I open the door to the stairway and peek down. It's all clear, so I creep down the three flights of stairs, and I make it to the first floor without incident. I'm breathing heavily, and my heart is racing. If I'm going to make it all the way down to Florida without having a heart attack, I need to calm down. Slowly, I open the door that leads into the lobby. Everything looks the same as always, but the absence of activity in the lobby is startling. Usually, there are nurses bustling about, and patients being checked in by the door. The front desk has a "Back in five minutes!" sign sitting on the counter. I have a feeling the receptionist won't be back in five minutes.

I move quickly across the lobby, and I almost jump out of my skin as the door to the front office swings open. A woman emerges, but she is turned away from me.

Short woman, brown hair, shuffling across the lobby, red shoes, feet dragging, shuffling across the lobby.

My tic is getting better. It used to be much worse. In my head, I would always recite the characteristics and actions of every single person I came across. Now I only do it when I'm startled or anxious. Dr. Emerson says my mental state is improving.

I can't tell if the shuffling woman has changed into a zombie yet. She is walking slowly at a strange angle, so I assume she's infected. I am amazed that she is not turning around to attack me. She's shuffling away, out the automatic sliding front door, and then she's gone.

I'll let her go for now. I stand by my rule to only kill zombies that are trying to attack. After all, they were like us once. With all of the medicine they have today, I'm sure scientists will find a cure, and then all the zombies can be turned back into humans. The trick is to stay alive in the meantime.

I make it to the front door without seeing any more zombies. I also don't see any humans, so I assume they're all hiding. That's the smartest thing to do. Just stay inside, lock up, and block all doors and windows. I, however, will not be staying inside. My mission in life has always been to save the world from zombies, and I can't do that if I'm hiding in my room like a coward.

I peek out the glass doors, careful not to step over the threshold that triggers the automatic door. There is no movement in my field of vision. I step directly in front of the door, and it opens to reveal a lone zombie about twenty yards away. Thankfully, my car is in the opposite direction. I sprint over to my silver 2004 Honda Civic. I slide in the car, throw my backpack on the passenger seat, start the engine, and peel out. My sister, Casey, gave me this car a few years ago. Her husband wanted her to drive a fancy German car, so I happily took her cast-off.

I drive toward Casey's house first, because I know she'll need my help more than my brother will. He's a police officer, and I know he can protect himself and his family. But I still need to stop by his house to pick up some supplies. I really hope Casey is home now. She's an elementary school teacher, but I doubt she went to work today. I have a mental image of seven-year-old zombies swarming the playground at her school. I shudder at the thought as I finish the short drive to Casey's house.

Jordan's Zombie Booklet Fact One

Zombies only eat human brains. They don't eat flesh or guts, just brains. The "experts" are still debating the zombie diet, but I know for a fact that zombies only eat brains.

Chapter 2

I pull up to Casey's house. Actually, with its huge, white columns, four-car garage, and elaborate garden complete with a koi pond, it's more of a mansion. Her house is way too big for just two people, but Greg, her husband, would consider any smaller house demeaning. All is quiet on Casey's street, so I walk up the long, stone path to her front door and knock quietly.

Casey opens the door almost immediately. "Jordan! I'm so glad you're here," she says.

Sweet face, dark hair, hiding a wound on her face, pink shirt, tear-filled eyes, hiding a wound on her face.

"What happened to your face?" I ask. Casey is the cute one in the family. She has a button nose, deep dimples, and big, brown eyes. Now, her perfect face is tainted by a huge gash on her right cheek. "Have you been bitten?"

"Oh no, I'm fine."

"Well, what happened?"

"Oh, I, uh, slammed my head in the car door."

"That's the dumbest thing I've ever heard. Why would you ever do that?" I ask as I follow her into her enormous living room. Everything is perfect in Casey's house, and I never want to touch anything for fear of breaking a priceless trinket. Greg collects expensive crap that he places around his house so everyone is sure to know how rich he is. One time when I was over for dinner, Casey dropped an expensive vase, which shattered and spilled water on a tiny corner of their Persian rug. Greg went berserk and screamed at Casey until his voice was hoarse, and then he sent me back to Gardner House before we even had dinner. He has serious issues, and I think he could benefit from a few therapy sessions with Dr. Emerson.

"It's not like I crushed my head on purpose. I was in a hurry to get in my car, and I accidentally slammed my head while I was trying to shut the door. It doesn't hurt anymore. I'm fine."

She's lying; I know it. I'm sure she had a run-in with a zombie. I really hope she hasn't been bitten. I give her a sad smile.

"Is Greg home?" I ask.

"No, he's still at work."

"Really? Are you sure it's wise for you to be alone? Maybe we should call him."

"No!" Casey practically yells. "He doesn't like to be disturbed while he's at work. He's very busy, and he hates it when I interrupt him. He says it costs him money every time I call."

Casey's husband is a patent attorney. He's obsessed with work, and he loves money more than a normal person should love anything. He previously worked for one of the biggest intellectual property law firms in the country, but he got greedy and stole several of their clients so he could open his own practice. Technically, what he did is legal, but it's pretty messed up. I wasn't surprised when I heard about the scandal. I think Greg was bullied a lot when he was a kid, but now that he finally has some power, he acts like a bully to everyone around him (except his clients).

"I know Greg's job is important," I say, "but he should be here with you. I'll just give him a quick call and see if he's able to leave work early just this one time." I would think that he could leave the office for the apocalypse. It seems like a good enough excuse to me.

"No, Jordan, he won't come home. I know he won't."

"You shouldn't be alone. I'm going over to Taylor's house now. Do you want to come with me?"

"No, that's OK. I think I'll just stay here and wait for Greg to get home."

I hope Greg does come home. "OK, Casey. Promise me that you'll call Taylor if you feel unsafe."

"Of course I will. Please don't worry about me. I'll be just fine."

That's what Casey always says. *I'll be just fine.* I hope she's right. I give my little sister a big hug before I head out the door. Lucky for me, there are no zombies around. I'm furious with myself for not getting here in time to save my sister. Her bite wound looked pretty serious, but maybe it's only a scratch. If it's just a scratch, she won't get infected.

The thought of my little sister turning into a zombie is devastating. As I climb into my car, I let out an involuntary sob, and then I push it back down and hold back the tears. I can't let anyone else get infected. I call my mom again, but the phone just rings. She really needs to get an answering machine. I speed off to Taylor's house, hoping that he is home.

My siblings and I have always been close. Before the accident, we had a charmed childhood. Our father died when we were young, but our mother raised us very well. She is a steadfast feminist, which is why she gave all three of her children unisex names. She wanted us to become writers, and she didn't want our writings to be judged based on our gender. She still loves us, even though not one of us is a published writer. I was hoping to publish my zombie fact booklet, and I'm disappointed that I didn't have a chance to get it out there before the zombies invaded.

Jordan's Zombie Booklet Fact Two

The only way for a human to change into a zombie is if he or she is bitten. A scratch from a zombie will not infect a human. Zombie saliva mixed with a victim's blood is what changes a person into a zombie. Even though zombies don't eat flesh, they still bite humans to incapacitate them. Obviously, if a zombie approaches you, do whatever you can to avoid being bitten.

CHAPTER 3

It takes me only fifteen minutes to get to Taylor's house. As I pull up next to his home, I see two cars in the driveway. He has a small, brick house that's just big enough for his family of four, but it's overflowing with a ton of stuff, things, possessions, crap. It's not Taylor's fault. His wife, Veronica, has a bit of a shopping problem. She used to be an office manager, but she decided to quit her job after she had her first baby. Now she shops to fill the time. I try to be nice to Veronica because she's my sister-in-law, but she's extremely shallow, which makes her difficult to be around.

Before getting out of the car, I look up and down my brother's street. I see zombies milling around at the end of the block, but I have plenty of time to get to the door before any of them can spot me. I quietly make my way to the front door and gingerly knock. The door swings open.

Tall woman, scared face, tripping on the step, blue shirt, foggy glasses, tripping on the step.

I catch Taylor's nanny as she stumbles into me.

"Hi, Annie," I say. "Is Taylor home?"

"No, he was supposed to be home today, but he got called into work because they needed backup in the city," she says with a lisp. In addition to her tongue ring, Annie has rings in her nose and eyebrow. Her piercings and blue-streaked hair make her look a little odd, but she's pretty good with the kids.

"Is Veronica home?" I ask.

"Yeah, she's upstairs. Will you please tell her that I'm leaving? I have a family emergency, and I have to go home."

"I understand," I say sympathetically. "I hope your family is OK. Be safe out there."

"I will. Thanks, Jordan." Annie smiles at me as she walks out the door. I make sure she gets to her car safely before closing and locking the front door.

I walk into the family room, and through the sliding glass doors, I see that Taylor's kids are running around outside in the sprinkler. I can't believe Annie let them go outside during a zombie invasion.

"Nanny of the year," I mumble. I hurry to the back door and yell to the kids, "Hey, guys, want to come inside and play with me?"

"Joe-dan!" Michael shrieks in delight. My four-year-old nephew clumsily runs over to me. He's small for his age, but I'm sure he'll have a growth spurt soon. With his goofy smile and big, brown eyes, Michael looks a lot like Taylor.

"Hey, buddy, how are you? Why don't you come and play inside? You, too, Owen," I say.

"I want to keep playing in the sprinkler," Owen says.

"I need you to come inside. NOW."

"Five more minutes."

Just as Owen runs through the sprinkler, a zombie comes around the back of the house. I dash into the backyard and pick up Owen. He protests as I drag him into the house and slam the door behind us. I lock it and pull the curtains over the door so the boys won't see the decaying zombie in their backyard.

"I wasn't done playing," Owen whines.

Owen is extremely spoiled, but it isn't really his fault, because he's accustomed to getting his way. Owen is seven years old, and he thinks he knows everything. With his black hair, green eyes, and constant scowl, he takes after his mother more than his father. I pick up two thin towels with pictures of cartoon characters on them and hand them to the boys.

"Do you know where your mommy is?" I ask them both.

"She's upstairs," Michael says. "She's sleeping, and she said not to wake her up."

"Annie says that Mommy is on anti-depressers," Owen chimes in. "They make her sleepy."

I don't think kids are supposed to know about that stuff. Heaven knows why Annie shared that with them. "Listen boys, why don't you go change your clothes and then play upstairs for a while?"

"No, I'm going to play in the sprinkler again," Owen says, and he starts to walk back outside.

"Nope, you're done for today, buddy," I say as I grab his arm. "I'll make you a deal; if you go upstairs now and get changed into some dry clothes, I'll let you each have a Popsicle."

Michael smiles, but Owen shakes his head. "Popsicles are for babies. I want coffee."

"Um, I don't think your parents would want you to have coffee," I say.

"Mom lets us have coffee. She lets us have anything we can reach on the counter, and I can get the coffee if I stand on a chair," Owen says proudly.

Well, that's just bad parenting.

"I'll tell you what, if you go upstairs right now, I'll make a latte for each of you," I lie to get them to go upstairs.

"Make mine vanilla," Owen orders.

This is why I don't have kids.

"Upstairs. NOW!"

Owen turns and runs up the stairs with Michael right behind him. Now that the boys are gone, I creep down to the basement to get what I came for. I move a curtain out of the way to reveal the door to Taylor's fallout shelter. He got drunk one night and told me his secret code to open the door of the shelter. I press 2-4-6-8, and the door slowly opens. Taylor has been preparing for the end of the world for at least ten years. His friends tease him about it, but I'm sure they wish they had shelters now. Taylor never believed me when I told him that zombies would be the cause of the apocalypse. He thought it would be an asteroid or a nuclear bomb. I can't wait to throw this in his face. I love being right.

I step inside the shelter and see that it hasn't changed since I was last in here a few months ago. There is a shelf packed with MREs, and four cots are set up against the wall. Taylor has even included a toilet and running water. I'm happy to know that my brother will have a safe haven in which to wait out the apocalypse.

There are two large shelves packed with weapons. I gaze longingly at the rows of guns, knives, and bats as I pull a plastic bag out of my back pocket. I grab a semi-automatic pistol from Taylor's collection. He has plenty of other guns, so I'm sure he won't miss this one. I also grab some extra bullets, just in case. I fill my bag with ten MREs so I'll have enough to eat for the rest of the week. It shouldn't take me more than a few days to get to Florida, but I have to be prepared for anything. As an afterthought, I grab one of Taylor's hip holsters for the pistol.

After my bag is filled with supplies, I walk back up to the first floor and put my borrowed goods by the front door. I have one more thing to do before I leave. I creep up the stairs, tiptoeing past the boy's room, and I knock on Veronica's bedroom door. I wait for an answer, but there is none. I slowly open the door and see Veronica in bed, lying on her back.

Short woman, slender body, snoring lightly, beautiful face, sad expression, snoring lightly.

Veronica is a gorgeous woman, but she tends to frown a lot. With her shiny, jet-black hair, green eyes, and olive skin, she looks like she could be an actress in a zombie movie. She would be one of those useless characters who run in circles, screaming, while being chased by zombies. I think Taylor married her because she's beautiful. It couldn't have been for her personality. I suppose they make a good couple. My brother is attractive but not very smart. I'm the brainy one in the family.

Anyway, Taylor's wife is very self-involved and terribly depressed. The pretty ones are usually unhappy. They expect everyone to be enamored of their beauty. How can a person be content when their happiness lies in someone else's hands, ready to be crushed at any moment? Ordinary-looking people are far superior, because they are forced to actually work hard to achieve their goals, instead of expecting people to fall all over themselves to help them.

I don't think Veronica particularly likes me, but that's OK. I'm not the type of person who needs to be liked. As long as she makes my brother happy, then she's OK with me.

I lightly shake Veronica awake. "Jordan?" she croaks. "What the hell are you doing here?"

"I came to check on you. Annie had to leave because of a family emergency."

"Damn," she says as she takes a prescription bottle from her nightstand and pops two pills in her mouth.

"Should you be taking those right now?"

She just glares at me and asks, "Is Taylor home?"

"No, he had to go into work. Did you know that your kids were playing alone in the backyard?"

"Yeah, they love that damn sprinkler."

"I sent them up here to play. They should be OK now. Have you been running drills with the boys? Do they know about the fallout shelter?"

"I have no idea. That's Taylor's thing. He's so sure the world is going to end during our lifetime, but all of those useless supplies are cutting into our budget," she says, her voice disdainful.

She doesn't know about the zombies. I guess that makes sense because she has been in a fog for the past few years. She is so useless; maybe she can just sleep through the zombie invasion. She rolls away from me and puts a pillow over her head. I guess that's my cue to leave. I walk downstairs and call Taylor's cell phone, willing him to pick up.

"Hey, Jordan, what's up?"

Thank goodness. "Will you be off duty soon?"

"I probably won't be home tonight. We have a lot going on here, and I'm not sure when I'll be home. I'll just ask Annie to stay there for the night."

"Annie had to leave," I say.

"How do you know that?" Taylor asks.

"I'm at your house. I came to check on the boys. Annie left right when I got here, because she had a family emergency."

"Damn. Is Veronica awake?"

"Sort of. I'll make sure she's conscious before I leave."

"Thanks, Jordan. You're a lifesaver. I'll try to make it home tonight."

"Sounds good. Be safe, OK?" I say.

"I'm always safe," Taylor says before hanging up.

I walk back upstairs and knock on Owen's door. "Hey guys, I need you to each fill a bag with enough clothes to last a week. Understand?"

"Yeah," the boys say. They don't get up though.

"Now, please," I say before I close the door behind me. I walk back to Veronica's room and try to shake her awake, but she doesn't stir. I guess I'll have to carry her down to the fallout shelter. She must only weigh 115 pounds, but I struggle with the weight as I pick her up. With much difficulty, I get her out the bedroom door and down the hall. As I pass Owen's room, I kick his door to get the boys moving. Hefting his bag of clothes, Michael follows me into the hallway.

"Where's your brother?" I ask.

"He says he wants to finish his game first," Michael says.

Owen needs to learn to respect his elders. I struggle down the stairs with Veronica in my arms, followed closely by Michael. I consider asking him to go back upstairs to get his brother, but I may only have time to save one of the boys.

"Why are you carrying Mommy?" Michael asks.

"She's sleepy, so I'm just taking her downstairs to take a nap."

I barely make it to the fallout shelter before my knees buckle under Veronica's weight. I set her down and punch in the code. The door opens, and I nudge Michael inside. I don't feel like picking up Veronica again, so I drag her into the shelter and then pull her body onto one of the cots. I tell Michael to sit on a cot and not touch anything while I get his brother. I know the guns are out of his reach, but I don't want him getting into anything else. I run back up the stairs and find Owen sitting on the floor in his room, playing with his toys.

"Did you get your bag of clothes?" I ask.

"You said I could have a latte if I came upstairs. I'll pack my clothes when you get my latte," Owen says.

This kid is such a brat. "Or you can get your clothes together now, and then I'll give you a latte when you come downstairs with me. Let's get your bag packed," I say.

I find his backpack and rummage through his closet. I grab seven shirts and a few pairs of pants. I go to his drawer and grab a handful of socks and underwear. That should do it.

"Your bag is packed; now let's get downstairs."

"I need to finish my game," Owen says.

I don't know the child abuse laws in Maryland, but I think it's OK to hit a kid if he's acting like a jerk. I have to restrain myself because I'm very close to knocking my nephew unconscious. I settle for grabbing his arm and dragging him down the stairs.

"I'm not done," Owen whines.

"You are now," I say. "You, Michael, and your mom are going to play apocalypse down in the fallout shelter."

"What's apoclips?"

"It's when the world ends, and everybody has to work together to stay alive."

"Can I have my latte first?"

"Let's get you down to the shelter, and then we'll figure out your beverage situation."

I punch in the code again. The door slowly opens to reveal Veronica passed out on a cot and Michael obediently sitting next to his mom. I wish all kids were like Michael. Owen walks directly over to the weapons.

"Nope," I say, "those are for adults. You can't touch those."

"Yes, I can," he says as he picks up a handgun. Thank goodness they aren't loaded. I hope.

I snatch the gun from Owen and put it on a higher shelf. I put the rest of the weapons on shelves that Owen can't reach.

"That's not fair," he says. "Where's my latte?"

"I'm about to get it. Calm down."

Owen sits down next to Michael and crosses his arms in a huff. After I finish putting the rest of the weapons out of their reach, I take a jigsaw puzzle from another shelf and hand it to Owen.

"Play with this. I'll be right back," I say.

As I leave, I hear Owen throw the puzzle on the floor. If he keeps acting like a brat, maybe he'll be able to wake up

Veronica. I go to the kitchen to find a snack for the boys. Taylor will be able to show them how to eat the MREs when he gets home, but I'll need to get something to hold them over. I know one thing: I won't be making any lattes.

I fill a bag with crackers and canned goods to stock the shelter. As an afterthought, I grab two Popsicles before heading back to the basement. I punch in the code again and open the door to find Owen jumping on Veronica's cot. She's stirring, but she's not fully awake. Good, it's better if she's conscious.

"Where's my latte?" Owen demands.

"You guys are all out of lattes. Here," I say as I toss a Popsicle to him. I hand the other Popsicle to Michael, who happily opens it and starts licking his treat. I give Michael a big hug and tell him to be safe. He smiles at me through a mouth full of green Popsicle juice.

I hear Owen unwrap his Popsicle as I leave the room. I don't look back as I close the door behind me. I decide to leave Taylor a note so he knows where to find his family. I write, "V, O & M in fs." Hopefully, he'll know it means that I left his family in the fallout shelter. I leave the note by the front door.

I peek out the front window, and I see that no one is on the street. I pick up my bag with my borrowed supplies, and take a deep breath before opening the front door. I sprint to my car, even though there is no one around. You never know when a zombie will pop out. I put my bag of goods on the seat next to me, and then I start the engine. Before starting out, I try to call my mom one more time, but she still doesn't pick up her phone. The battery on my cell is running low, so I turn it off and put it in the glove compartment. I'll try to call her later this evening. If the traffic isn't bad, I should make it to Florida by tomorrow night.

Jordan's Zombie Booklet Fact Three

Zombies love keys. Whenever they see a human fumbling with keys, they know they'll be feasting on brains in the near future. If you're going to leave your car for less than ten minutes, leave your doors unlocked. If you're just stepping out of your house for a moment, leave your front door unlocked. Don't bother with keys, because they'll just get you killed.

Chapter 4

If I avoid highways, the drive to Jacksonville should take about seventeen hours. In zombie movies, without fail, highways are a nightmare. Everyone gets on the highways, and the first person to run out of gas or break down screws up everything.

I want to drive through most of the night, and I might try to get a few hours of sleep in the early morning. Most people would think zombies are more active at night, but it's just the opposite. Zombies don't sleep, but they do need to rest, and they usually take breaks at night. It's much safer for people to travel after dark. I pass the exit for the beltway, and there is a seemingly endless line of cars trying to get on the ramp from Old Georgetown Road. After I zoom past the beltway exit, I notice a man walking on the side of the road.

Tall man, broad shoulders, sticking his thumb out, dark hair, shabby clothes, sticking his thumb out.

He doesn't seem to be infected. I'm excited that I found the first person I can help. I pull my car over next to the man and roll down the window.

"Where are you headed?" I ask him.

"Richmond, Virginia," he says, leaning his head in the window.

"Great, hop in. I'm going right past Richmond."

"Thanks," he says as he gets in the car. With his thinning, gray hair and deep wrinkles on his forehead, I think he's probably in his late fifties. Despite all this, it looks like he's in great shape; his tight T-shirt barely contains his massive biceps.

"I suppose I should have asked you this first: have you been bitten, or have you run into any of the infected ones?" I say.

"No, I'm fine." He looks at me suspiciously. "Have you been bitten?"

"No. I've been lucky so far."

"That's good. I'm glad to hear it."

"So what's your name?" I ask the man.

"John," he says.

"I'm Jordan. It's nice to meet you. I'm glad I saw you. It's not safe for you to be walking around by yourself."

He doesn't respond.

"So where are you from?" I ask.

"Baltimore."

I wait for him to ask me where I'm from, but he doesn't say anything else. This guy isn't very chatty. I can't stand awkward silences, so I continue. "Baltimore is nice. I live in Rockville."

John doesn't respond. He's just looking out the window. I'll bet he's in shock because of the whole zombie thing, but I know how to get him talking.

"I live in a psychiatric hospital," I say.

His head whips around, and I see him studying my face. "You live in an insane asylum?"

"We prefer that people refer to it as a psychiatric hospital. But, yes, I live in an insane asylum."

"Why were you committed?"

"I wasn't committed. I live there voluntarily. It's nice there, and they take good care of us." I'm glad I finally got him talking.

"So, uh, are you crazy, or something?"

"Not really. I just have a common disorder. It's not a big deal."

"What kind of disorder?" John asks.

"Middle Child Syndrome," I say with a straight face.

"Really? That's odd. I didn't know that was a real disorder."

This guy has no idea that I'm kidding. People assume that I don't have a sense of humor just because I'm a little crazy.

"Oh, sure, Middle Child Syndrome is quite common," I continue. "It's a very serious problem, and it should be treated immediately when symptoms arise."

"What are the symptoms?"

"Jealousy, rage, severe headaches, hysteria, seizures, and pink eye."

"Pink eye?" he asks skeptically.

"Sure, it happens all the time." I'm about to elaborate on my lie when I see a man on the side of the road up ahead, standing by a red station wagon.

Short man, skinny man, waving at me, black jacket, sunken eyes, waving at me.

As I slow down to get a better look at the man who's signaling for me to pull over, I see two little girls playing next to a stand of trees. I hadn't even realized that we left the city and entered the suburbs. There is a development of houses across the way and a forest on our side of the road. The man says something to the girls, and they get a little closer to him. What is wrong with this man? Those kids should be in the car, not standing next to a dark forest where a zombie could pop out and attack them at any moment.

"I'm just going to see what they need," I say to John. I pull over and turn off the car.

"You gonna pick them up, too?"

"If I have to, I will. I'm going to leave the keys in the ignition so we can make a quick getaway, if necessary. Leave the doors unlocked. I'll be back in a few minutes."

"OK," John says.

I approach the man, and as I get closer I notice that his skin is extremely pale. His face is sweating, and he looks like he's running a fever. He hasn't turned yet, but it's obvious he's been bitten, and it won't be long before he's a zombie.

Jordan's Zombie Booklet Fact Four

> Zombies shuffle. They don't speed-walk, and they certainly don't run. I am always annoyed by movies that show zombies sprinting after humans. It's just not possible.

Chapter 5

"Are you OK?" I ask the sickly looking man.

"I got a flat tire, and I don't have a spare. I'm only five miles from home," he says.

"I've got a spare that you can have. Let me just grab it, and I'll be right back." I walk to my car and open the driver's side door so I can pop the trunk. John jumps when I open the door, and I just grin at him. He's definitely scared of me. It's more useful to have someone fear you than respect you. I wink at John and close the door, and then I grab my spare and a jack from the trunk.

"Thank you so much. You're a lifesaver," the man says as I hand him the spare.

This man is beyond saving, but maybe I can save his kids if I can get them away from him. If he changes into a zombie while they're with him, those little girls won't stand a chance. I hear one of the girls scream, and I put my hand on my gun as I race around the car to get a better shot.

"Heather, stop it," the man says. "I told you not to put your little sister in a headlock."

"Laura started it," she says.

"Enough! Now let go of your sister and get back here."

"You should probably have them stand by the car," I suggest. "It's not safe for them to be by the woods."

"They're fine. There's no one around. You're the first person we've seen."

"I know, but don't you think they'd be safer by the car?"

"They're fine," he says again. It's obvious that he's getting annoyed with me.

He bends down to start jacking up the car, but he's having a lot of trouble. He stands up to wipe his brow, and then he bends down again to start over.

"I can do it," I say.

"No, I'm fine. I've just been under the weather lately," he says. "I just need a minute."

The man starts coughing and then heaves for a few seconds. I take the jack from him; he doesn't argue.

I have the flat tire off in less than two minutes, and I'm putting the spare on when I say, "You said your house is only five miles from here?"

"Yes. Well, their mother's house is five miles from here. I don't live there anymore. I'm just dropping off my kids."

I get it. He wants to make sure his kids are safely away from him when he turns into a zombie. If I had the courage, I would take this man's kids and drive off. But I don't know where their mother lives, and I can't be traveling with two little girls. I decide to follow them and make sure they make it to their mother's house safely. I'll be able to defend them if their father turns into a zombie while they're on the road.

"Well, you better get out of here," I say to him.

"Thanks for the tire. I appreciate it."

"No problem." I'm about to give him one of my zombie fact booklets, but I suppose it won't be of much use to him.

As his kids are getting in the car, I give one of my booklets to Heather. She looks like she's about ten years old, so I assume she can read.

"Thanks," she says. I hear her sister ask her what it is as she gets in the car. "I think it's a comic book," Heather says.

Hopefully, the "comic book" will be useful to those girls and their mother. I get back in my car, and I tell John that we're going to make a quick detour. He grimaces. I can tell that he's not thrilled, but he doesn't have a choice. After a few miles of following the family's car at a safe distance, John asks what I'm doing.

"I need to make sure those kids are OK. He's dropping them off at their mother's house, and I need to confirm that they make it safely. I'm not sure he'll be able to make it all the way home," I say.

"That's nice of you. Are you a Good Samaritan, or something?"

"I suppose you could call it that. I'm just trying to do my part to save the world. I think if everyone helped out, we could get out of this mess more smoothly."

"I agree. There are a lot of awful people out there, and it's nice to meet a Good Samaritan. Even if you are a little crazy," he smiles.

I'm about to tell John about my booklet when I see the family pull onto a side street. I follow them, trying to be inconspicuous. They turn into a cul-de-sac that has four huge, brick houses that look exactly alike, and they pull up next to a long driveway. The kids hop out of the back seat, but their father stays in the car. I can't believe he's just letting them walk to the front door by themselves. Maybe he's already starting to turn.

The girls are making their way to the front door when I see a zombie coming around the side of the house in the shadows. As the walking corpse shuffles toward the girls, I notice that he has a gaping hole in his chest and one of his arms is missing. In a flash, I'm out of my car with my gun in my hand. The zombie is approaching the kids from behind, but they don't notice. They're almost to the front door when it swings open, and a woman, who I assume is their mother, ushers them inside. Thank goodness. I didn't want to have to spray this zombie's brains all over the pavement in front of those kids. I'm sure they're going to go through enough over the next few days.

Hopefully, I'll make it through the day without having to kill anything. I get back in the car as the kids' father drives off in the opposite direction. I guess he hasn't turned yet.

"What was that all about?" John asks.

"Oh, I just wanted to make sure the kids got inside safely."

"I see," he says. He gives me an inquisitive look. "You think we can get back on the road now?"

"Of course," I say.

That's a good idea. It's almost 8:00, and it's starting to get dark. Hopefully, the zombies won't be too active tonight.

Just when I think it will be smooth sailing for the rest of the evening, we drive past an outlet mall with zombies swarming the parking lot. I hope there are no people there. If there are, they won't be alive for long. I zoom past the outlet mall, wishing them luck. Even I can't take on that many zombies.

Jordan's Zombie Booklet Fact Five

Once a person is bitten, it can take anywhere from a few hours to a few days to turn into a zombie. It depends on where the bite is and how severe it is. If family members or friends are bitten, put them in an isolated area where they can't hurt anyone. You don't have to kill them, because there may be a cure, and there's a chance your loved ones could be saved. Make sure they're in a secure location where they can't get out and harm anyone.

Chapter 6

We don't spot any more zombies on our drive to Richmond. I know they're out there, but they must have settled down for the night. We're almost to Richmond when I ask John where he wants me to drop him off.

"My cousin lives over on West Nineteenth Street," he says. "You think you can drop me off there?"

"Sure, no problem," I say. "That's nice that you're going to be with family."

"Yeah," John says. He's hasn't talked much in the past two hours. "Make a left up here, and his house is on the right," he says.

"You got it," I say.

I turn onto West Nineteenth Street and gaze at the old, dilapidated row houses on the block. There is no one on the street, so I assume the city is on lockdown. I notice that it's almost 11:00 as I pull up outside of John's cousin's house.

He hops out of the car. "Thanks for the ride," John says. "Be safe."

"I will," I say. "Oh, wait, I almost forgot." I give a booklet to John. "This should help keep you safe."

John looks at the booklet and puts it in his pocket. He smiles, and says, "Thanks."

I stay where I am until he makes it safely inside, and then I drive back the way I came. I'm starting to get tired, but I know I need to stay awake for at least a few more hours. If I'm going to make it to Jacksonville by tomorrow night, I'll have to drive for as long as possible.

As I leave the city limits of Richmond, I notice a convenience store with a huge, red sign, with the words "Rosco's Food and Gas" above the door. The store seems to be closed, but I see a figure standing outside the store, peering in the front window. I don't think it's a zombie, but I can't be sure. This might be a trap, but if it's not, this person looks like she needs help.

I drive past the convenience store, and the figure turns toward me when my headlights shine in that direction. I look at the person in my rearview mirror, and I know that she is definitely not a zombie. I get out of my car, and I walk over to the woman.

Tall woman, curly hair, backing away from me, torn clothes, wide eyes, backing away from me.

"Hey," I say. "Do you need help with something?"

The woman doesn't look happy to see me. I would guess that she has been wearing the same outfit for days. Her red, plaid shirt is stained, and her jeans are torn, but not in a fashionable way. Her long, dark hair looks like it hasn't been washed for a long time, and her face could use a good scrub. She turns away from me and glances longingly in the store window.

"I have some MREs in my car, if you want a couple," I say.

"You got drugs?" she asks, her voice hopeful.

"MREs aren't drugs," I laugh. "They are 'Meals Ready to Eat,' and I have plenty in my car."

"Thanks, but I actually have my eye on those cigarettes." She looks longingly at the display in the window.

"Oh, well, I guess the shop owner won't miss them," I say.

I can tell that she thinks I'm judging her. "Normally, I don't steal, but I've been having a hard time lately," she explains.

"I completely understand. I think everyone is going through a rough period right now. I'm going to get you those cigarettes. Stand back." I take my gun out of my hip holster, and, before the woman has a chance to say anything, I fire two shots at the front window. The glass shatters easily. I expect to hear an alarm, but it's completely silent inside. The power is probably already out in this area.

"Get your cigarettes. I'll stay out here and keep watch," I say.

"Thanks."

"Be quick about it. We don't want any unwanted visitors showing up."

"You got it."

I see her grab a basket and add four cartons of cigarettes. It looks like someone has a smoking problem. On the bright side, I guess the probability of dying of lung cancer is slim these days. Death by a zombie bite is much more likely. I turn back to the street. I know that zombies are attracted to noise, but I'm hoping that there aren't any in the area. I look back over my shoulder, and the woman is taking her time gathering food. She better hurry up because I'm starting to freak out a bit. I hate being out in the open like this.

Finally, she climbs back out of the store. "Thanks again." She smiles at me. "Do you want anything?" she asks, pointing at her basket.

"No, thanks, I don't smoke, and I have plenty of food. Do you need a ride somewhere?"

She pauses, and it looks like she is considering accepting my offer. Then she glances at my gun, and I can tell she's uncomfortable.

"I could protect you," I blurt out.

"No, I'm OK. Thanks for the offer," she says. She turns away and starts to walk quickly in the other direction. "Thanks for everything," she tosses over her shoulder. She disappears into the darkness with her basket of loot.

I definitely freaked her out, but at least I was able to help her get some food. I realize that I forgot to give her a booklet. Hopefully, she won't need it. I get back in my car and see that it's almost 11:30, and I decide to drive for at least two more hours. My eyes are already starting to feel heavy, but I want to cover as much ground as possible.

Jordan's Zombie Booklet Fact Six

Zombies do not have superhuman strength. If anything, zombies are weaker than humans. Their bodies are decaying, so they aren't very difficult to kill. I recommend that you always carry a weapon with you. Even though zombies are weak, you don't want to get close enough to have a fistfight with one, because a zombie bite will infect and kill you.

Chapter 7

I pull into a campground at 1:57 a.m. I almost drove off the road a few times, so I know it's time for me to stop. I made it through Virginia and into North Carolina, and that's far enough for one night. I pull into a clearing, and I see three people sitting around a campfire. They should know better. It's like they're ringing a dinner bell for all the zombies in the area. I park about twenty yards away from the campers, and then I get out of my car and walk over to the group.

One woman, two men, laughing loudly, red faces, glazed eyes, laughing loudly.

"Hey, there," I say. "Do you mind sharing your campground for the night?"

"Not at all," the first guy says. He has huge muscles, and there doesn't appear to be an ounce of fat on him. I'm guessing he's about 6'5". He seems friendly, but I wouldn't want to get on his bad side.

"Great," I say as I sit down next to the giant man. "Are you sure it's a good idea to have a campfire right now?"

"It's perfectly safe," the second man says curtly. He's considerably smaller than the other man, but for some reason, he's more intimidating. There is something in his eyes that makes him seem creepy.

"Why don't you join us for a drink?" the woman says. She's fairly attractive, with short, blonde hair, and blue eyes. She doesn't look like she belongs with these two scruffy men.

"I'm pretty tired," I say.

"Just one drink; it'll help you sleep better," she says.

I don't accept her offer right away, because I don't drink much. Well, I don't drink at all, but I don't want to be rude. "OK, I'll join you for one drink." I'm not going to drink, but I'll sit with them until they put out their campfire. I know we're all in danger, so I'm glad I'm prepared for a zombie attack.

"I'm Sarah," the woman says. She points at the large man, "This is Sander, and this lovely gentleman is David," she says, indicating the creepy man. He doesn't look lovely to me.

"It's nice to meet you all. I'm Jordan." The woman looks like she's in her early twenties, and I'm guessing that Sander and David are in their late twenties. "Where are you guys from?" I ask.

"I'm from Virginia," Sarah answers. "I was heading south when I ran into Sander and David. They're on their way to South Carolina, and they were nice enough to give me a ride. Where are you from?"

"I'm from Maryland, but I'm heading down to Florida. I have to make sure my mom is all right."

"That's nice of you," Sarah says. She hands me a strong-smelling drink. "I like your shirt."

I look down. I forgot that I put on my "Zombie Slayer" T-shirt this morning.

"Thanks," I grin. "I don't want you to get the wrong idea about me. I only kill zombies that are trying to attack humans. I don't slaughter zombies for fun. They were just like us once, and I firmly believe in zombies' rights."

Sarah nervously laughs. "You're crazy."

"I know," I say. "That's why I live in a psychiatric hospital."

Three heads snap up and stare at me. I love doing that. People get really freaked out when I tell them that I live in a mental hospital. It's one of the many perks of living at Gardner House.

"Why do you live in a psychiatric hospital?" Sander asks. "Are you a lunatic?"

"No, I'm just a little crazy."

"Were you born crazy, or did you become crazy?" Sarah asks.

No one has ever asked me that before.

"I don't think I was born crazy, so I must have turned crazy," I reason.

"What happened?" she asks.

"I murdered an old man while he was in his bed," I say.

Sarah gasps and hides behind David.

"I didn't know what to do with the body," I say with a sly grin, "so I chopped it up and hid it under the floorboards in his room. When the police came to investigate, I played it cool at first, but I could hear the old man's heartbeat coming from beneath the floorboards. It drove me crazy, and I couldn't take it anymore, so I confessed to the murder."

"Wait," Sander says, "that sounds familiar."

"You probably heard about it on the news," I say.

"That's not it," Sander says. "Isn't that the plot of 'The Tell-Tale Heart' by Edgar Allan Poe?"

Busted.

The three of them stare at me like I'm completely insane.

"Interesting fact," I say to break the silence, "the story of 'The Tell-Tale Heart' is narrated in first person, and the protagonist's gender is never revealed. Most people assume the murderer is a man, but it's possible the killer is a woman."

"That's ridiculous," David says. "The murderer is obviously a man."

"Not necessarily. Maybe the murderer was a woman, and she killed the old man because she was fed up with him and his nasty, vulture-like eye. Either way, no one can confirm the gender of the murderer in 'The Tell-Tale Heart,'" I say.

"That's so stupid. Why would anyone write a story without revealing the main character's gender?" David says.

This guy is so narrow-minded.

"I think it's fascinating that the killer's gender is never revealed," I say. "In horror stories, gender stereotypes are usually exaggerated to the point that the story isn't enjoyable. The rage-filled killer is almost always a man, and the victim is most likely a dim-witted blonde with the mental capacity of a pea. It's refreshing to read a horror story that doesn't play into gender stereotypes. Don't you think?"

"Who wants to do shots?" David asks.

"Me!" Sarah says gleefully.

"I'm really tired," I say. "I think I'll just go to bed." I put my full cup down and walk away from the group. They don't try to stop me.

I get in the front seat of my car and lock the doors. I lean back and immediately fall asleep. I have a vivid dream that the dead man from 'The Tell-Tale Heart' turns into a zombie and comes after me. His eyes have popped out of their sockets, and he has pieces of bloody flesh hanging from his mouth. I try to drive away from him, but my car won't start. Then, all of a sudden, my car is gone, and the dead man is standing right in front of me. I reach for my gun, but that's gone too, and I have no way to defend myself. As he gets closer, I realize that it isn't the dead man with the vulture-like eye. It's my mother, and she wants to kill me.

I am jolted awake by a loud tapping noise. I look up and see a woman standing at the window on the passenger side of my car. I rub my eyes and realize that it's Sarah from last night. She taps my window again and gestures for me to roll it down. I start my car so I can comply.

"Hey," she smiles, "can you give me lift?"

"What happened to your two friends?" I ask.

"They took off this morning, and they stole my bag. I have nothing left. They got my wallet, my phone, and all my belongings."

"Well, that sucks," I say. I unlock the doors, "Hop in this car so the crazy person can give you a ride."

She hesitates, but then she thanks me and climbs in.

"Why are you headed to South Carolina?" I ask.

"I ran out of money, so I'm going down to see if my sister will take me in."

"I'm sure she will."

"You don't know my sister. She's not a generous person, but she's the only family I have left."

"I think it's great that you're going to be with your sister. Family is all we have during these difficult times."

"I guess. I appreciate you giving me a ride," she says. "I think I'm going to try to take a nap. I didn't get much sleep last night, if you know what I mean."

"I know exactly what you mean. I have nightmares too. You get some sleep, and I'll drive for as long as I can."

"Thanks," she says. She gives me a strange look and then turns her head away from me.

I drive until I need to make a pit stop then I pull over at a rest area. I nudge Sarah, but she seems to be in a deep sleep. I leave the car on so she doesn't have to be in here without the air conditioning. I grab my backpack and a change of clothes. I feel grimy from being in the car for so long. I walk to the bathroom with my gun at the ready. I'm always prepared for a zombie to pop out. After I confirm there are no zombies in the restroom, I relieve myself, change my clothes, and then wash my hands and splash cold water on my face. I'm feeling much better as I walk back to the car.

I hear my car start and notice Sarah in the driver's seat. I guess she wants to drive for the next leg of the trip. I'm walking around to the passenger side when the car is thrown into reverse. I frantically wave my arms at Sarah as she puts the car into drive and speeds off.

Jordan's Zombie Booklet Fact Seven

Zombies don't have extremely sensitive hearing. They are attracted to loud noises, but their hearing abilities are the same as humans. If a zombie is around, keep quiet and hope that they don't smell you. Zombies do have a keen sense of smell. Human flesh is enticing to zombies, and they track people using their sense of smell.

CHAPTER 8

"You forgot me!" I yell as Sarah disappears around the corner. I don't understand. I was perfectly willing to share my car with her. That's typical. Some people can't stand sharing; they want everything for themselves. Now I'm out here alone, without a car, deprived of all my survival supplies. I check the contents of my backpack and find that I have one MRE, one bottle of water, and yesterday's dirty clothes.

I suppose panicking would just be a waste of time, so I start walking south, trying not to freak out. I need to stay positive. Jacksonville can't be that far away. My map is in the car, but I know that I'm somewhere in South Carolina. I just need to make it through Georgia, and I'll be fine.

I take in my surroundings as I'm walking, and there isn't much life in this rural area. I pass a rundown farmhouse, but I decide not to risk checking it out. I've watched *Night of the Living Dead* countless times, and I know what happens to farmhouses in zombie movies (it's not good). After walking for half an hour, I decide that I will need to find a ride somehow. Every little sound makes me jump, and I won't be able to walk all the way to Jacksonville like this. I trudge along a one-lane road until I come across a sign for a highway. I expect it to be packed with cars, but as I reach the interstate, I see only three cars go by. Not one of them slows down to look at me. Maybe I should try smiling at passing cars so people will know I'm a human. I'm sure everyone assumes I'm a zombie, because who in their right mind would be walking along a highway during a zombie invasion? I run into some luck when a pickup truck pulls up next to me. The window on the passenger side rolls down.

Two men, greasy hair, grinning at me, plaid shirts, bloodshot eyes, grinning at me.

"Where you headed?" the driver leans over and asks.

"I'm on my way to Jacksonville. My car was stolen, and I would really appreciate a ride," I say.

"There ain't much room up front," the driver says. "How's 'bout ya get in the truck bed?"

"Great. Thanks!" I say as I clumsily climb into the back of the truck. It's not ideal, but I'm grateful that I don't have to walk anymore. I find a marginally comfortable position, and almost immediately, I fall asleep.

* * *

I'm jostled awake, and it takes a moment for me to realize where I am, and why I'm in the back of a truck. I check my watch and am surprised that it's 1:00 p.m. I can't believe I slept for almost three hours. We must be somewhere is northern Georgia. I wonder why we're on a back road. Maybe we encountered some zombies while I was sleeping.

I feel guilty that I wasn't awake to help out, so I'll have to apologize later.

The truck comes to a stop in a clearing. I see a log cabin about twenty yards away, surrounded by a group of trees. There are no other houses around, and I have no idea where we are. Both doors of the truck open at the same time, and the two men emerge. I stand up and hop out of the truck bed.

"Thank you so much for the ride," I say. "I'm sorry I fell asleep. Where are we?"

The driver answers with a different question, "What's in your backpack?" He's an obese man with a long, dark beard and beady eyes.

"Not much. I have a bottle of water and an MRE. And my dirty clothes from yesterday."

"How's 'bout ya hand it over?" the driver demands.

"Oh, sure, there isn't much, but I'm willing to share," I say as I pass the backpack over to the man who was in the passenger seat. He's quite short compared to the driver, and I notice that he doesn't have a single tooth in his entire mouth. I've never seen that before on a grown person. He probably wouldn't be a very successful zombie without any teeth. I'll bet he would starve to death within days.

I snap back to reality when the driver asks if I have a wallet. I'm getting a bad feeling about this.

"Sure, I have a wallet. There isn't much money in it. I think I only have ten dollars. I know money isn't going to help anyone these days." I'm babbling. I do that when I'm nervous.

"Toss it over so we can take a look," the driver says. I toss my wallet over to the passenger, and he opens it.

"Yep, only ten dollars in here," he says.

"Got anything else on ya?" the driver asks.

I instinctively put my hand on my gun. I can't let them have my only weapon. Without my gun, I'll be dead by the end of the day.

"What's that ya got there?" the driver asks.

I draw the gun and aim it at him. The two men put their hands in the air. "I appreciate you giving me a ride, but I think I'll be going now. I'd like my backpack, please." I point the gun at the passenger. He looks at the driver as if asking for permission, and the driver nods at him.

The passenger tosses the backpack at my feet, but I don't move a muscle. I still have my gun pointed at the toothless man. "I'd like my wallet, too, Deliverance."

The passenger doesn't even look at the driver for permission. He just tosses the wallet at my feet. Without taking my eyes or my gun off the two men, I bend down to pick up my wallet and backpack.

"Thank you again for the ride. I have to say, it really isn't right to steal. I know these are difficult times, but people need to stick together if they want to survive."

The driver spits in my general direction.

Charming.

My gun is still pointed at them as I back away. I continue to back up until the men are out of sight, then I turn and run at full speed with my gun still in my hand. I sprint until I know I'm far enough away that those men won't catch me. I slow my run to a jog, and then, when I'm out of breath, I start to walk. I'm surrounded by massive live oak trees, and I can only see snippets of the sky. I have no idea if I'm walking south, but I don't care right now. I just want to put some distance between me and those vile men. I keep tripping over pinecones, and I need to be careful because I'll be in a lot of trouble if I fall and twist my ankle. After an hour of stumbling through the forest, I finally get to a two-lane road.

I pull my water bottle from my backpack and take a big gulp. I know I need to conserve my water, but I think I've earned an extra sip. Thank goodness I got my backpack back from those men. I would not last the rest of the day without food and water. That's when I realize that I haven't eaten since yesterday morning. If I'm going to walk for the rest of the day, I'll need to eat something, so I decide to eat half of my MRE.

I'm walking beside the road, munching on some peanut butter crackers when I hear a rustling sound nearby. I would feel better walking in the forest where I wouldn't be as out in the open, but I need to follow the road so I'm sure that I'm walking south. I had a fancy compass for my trip, but I left it in my car. Now Sarah has a fancy compass. I wonder where she is right now. She's probably all safe and cozy at her sister's house, while I'm walking along the edge of a forest, rationing my last bit of food.

A car zooms by without stopping, but I don't have my thumb out this time. I'm done with hitchhiking. By 4:30 in the afternoon, my food and water are gone. I'm exhausted and thirsty, and I really don't know what to do. I'm not sure how much longer I can go on like this. I know I'm going to have to find a place to camp, but I'm not ready for that just yet.

I walk for another half hour until my feet can't take it anymore. Fortunately, I see a small town about two hundred yards ahead. I cautiously walk toward the town center. Lining what looks like the town's main street are tiny shops with darkened window displays featuring items that are completely useless now that the zombies have invaded. A giant stuffed frog in the window of a candy shop catches my eye, and for a moment, I consider breaking into the candy store. I would die for some Twizzlers, but I decide against raiding the sweet shop because I see a store at the end of the street with its lights on and an "Open" sign in the window. The sign above the door says, "Christian Science Reading Room."

Jordan's Zombie Booklet Fact Eight

The only way to kill a zombie is to destroy its brain. A gunshot to the head will do the trick. Or you can bash in a zombie's brain with a blunt object, but that's more labor intensive.

Chapter 9

This seems like a bit of good luck. It would be nice to meet a good Christian person. I walk into the Reading Room and see a slim woman who looks like she is in her seventies.

Tiny woman, smiling face, shuffling toward me, pink sweatshirt, kind eyes, shuffling toward me.

"Hello, dear, we're about to close, but I can give you some literature to take with you."

Literature?

"I was actually hoping I could bother you for some water," I say. "I have been traveling all day, and I'm very thirsty."

"Well, of course, dear. Let me get some for you in the back." I notice that she has piercing, blue eyes beneath massive glasses that cover the entire top half of her face. I didn't know they made glasses that big.

"Thanks," I say, handing her my empty water bottle.

"While you're waiting, feel free to look at some literature," she says before meandering into the back room.

This woman really loves her literature. I stand awkwardly in the middle of the small room until she returns with my water bottle. She hands it to me, and I finish all of the water in three gulps.

"Thanks," I say. "May I please have a refill?"

"You sure are thirsty," she smiles as she takes my water bottle and disappears into the back room.

I'm left alone with the literature again. You can barely see the walls because there are three massive bookshelves brimming with books and pamphlets. I look down at an open booklet sitting on a short, wooden desk next to me. I give into my curiosity and read the subject line, "Ancient and Modern Necromancy, Alias Mesmerism and Hypnotism, Denounced." Maybe this woman has known all along that the zombies would be coming. She might be an asset.

"Here you are, dear," the woman says, startling me as she returns with my water.

"Thanks again." I take a gulp from the water bottle and put the rest in my backpack for later.

"Where are you from?" the woman asks.

"Maryland. I'm trying to reach my mom in Jacksonville, Florida. I have to make sure she's OK."

"I'm sure she's fine, dear. You look exhausted. Have you been driving all day?"

"Walking, actually. My car was stolen this morning."

"How awful! Did you call the police?"

"No, I'm sure they have more important matters to deal with." I pause. "Where are we exactly? I got a little lost today."

"This is Garden City, Georgia. We're just north of Savannah," she says. "You're not very far from Jacksonville. You can probably take a bus the rest of the way."

This town must be very sheltered because this woman doesn't seem to know how bad it is out there. You should never rely on public transportation during the apocalypse. Everyone should know that.

"I'm not really a fan of buses. I'll find somewhere to camp for the rest of the night, and then I'll walk as far as I can tomorrow."

"Don't be silly, dear. You can stay at my home tonight. We're having beef barley stew for dinner."

My stomach gurgles with pleasure at the thought of stew. I would kill for a warm meal. "That sounds great," I say to the woman, "but I hate to impose."

"You wouldn't be imposing. I insist you stay the night. Let me just lock up the Reading Room, and then we can go. I don't live too far from here."

We walk outside, and I'm surprised when the woman continues to walk down the block.

"You didn't drive?" I ask her.

"Oh, no, I only live about a half mile away," she says. "It's good to walk. It keeps me healthy. Plus, I don't drive much these days."

"I see," I say. I don't like the idea of this little woman walking around town by herself. I'm glad I'm here to protect her. We pass several small houses with boarded up windows and doors, so I'm glad to know that some people in this town are taking precautions.

We stroll along in silence, and I'm not really sure what to talk about. I consider saying, "So…how about that annoying ancient and modern necromancy?" But that's not exactly a great way to start a conversation.

The woman spares me from starting the exchange on the wrong foot. "What's your name, dear?" she asks.

"Jordan. What's yours?"

"My name is Doris Dolores Dittmore."
I chuckle.
She looks hurt. Oh, I thought she was kidding.
"I am named after both of my grandmothers," she explains. "You can call me Doris."
"Oh, that's nice. Sorry I laughed. I can't help it. I'm kind of crazy," I explain.
"That's OK, dear. Everyone is a little crazy sometimes."
"No, I'm actually crazy," I say. "I live in a psychiatric hospital."
"Well, I hope they take good care of you there," she says.
She pats my arm and smiles. Doris is the first person I've met who hasn't asked me why I live in a mental hospital. I think I'm going to like her. We continue to walk in silence.
"So…" I mumble, "what do you think about this ancient and modern necromancy that's going around?"
"Hmmm? What's that, dear?" Doris asks.
"Nothing, I was just commenting on the weather."
"Oh, yes, it's very nice out today."
We arrive at a cottage with shabby shutters and a blue door that needs repainting. It's a one-story house. A Cape Cod, I think they call it. Or maybe it's a bungalow. I actually have no idea what kind of house it is. Doris unlocks the door, and we step into her home. There are three small rooms visible from the front hallway. I peer into the tiny kitchen and smile when I see the outdated, green appliances that must be from the 1970s, and then I glance at the miniscule dining room that barely has room for the wooden table and four mismatched chairs. I look into the living room and jump when I notice a sickly looking man sitting in a recliner.

Pale skin, gray hair, straining to sit up, hollow face, cloudy eyes, straining to sit up.

He has three blankets covering him, but he still looks cold. I can't help noticing how pale his skin looks. We could be in a lot of trouble. I'm fairly certain this man has been bitten, and it won't be long before he turns.

"This is my husband, Howard," Doris says. "Howard, this is Jordan." Howard strains to hold up his hand to greet me. I'm not really sure what to do, so I wave at him and smile.

"I'll show you the guest room so you can put your belongings down and get settled," Doris says. She takes me into a narrow hallway that has three closed doors. She points to the first door, "That's my room." Doris gestures to the second door, "That's the bathroom. We only have one bathroom in the house, but I'm sure you won't mind sharing."

"Not at all," I say. "I'm so grateful that you're letting me stay here."

"Naturally, we couldn't let you sleep outside. That wouldn't be safe." That's an understatement. She points to the third door, "And this will be your room for the night. Get washed up and comfortable. Dinner will be ready in about ten minutes."

I take the fastest shower in history, and then I quickly wash yesterday's dirty clothes in the bathroom sink. I hope Doris won't mind. I'll have to wear dirty clothes to dinner, but I'll wash them before I go to bed so I'll have two sets of clean clothes for tomorrow.

I emerge from my room, and a heavenly scent hits my nostrils. I haven't eaten a proper meal in days, so I would eat just about anything right now, but that beef barley stew smells scrumptious. I walk into the cozy dining room and seat myself on a dark, wooden chair that clashes with the light, wooden table. Doris sets a large bowl of stew in front of me and then she sits down on a white chair that looks like it has seen better days.

"Shall we pray?" Doris says.

"Oh, sure," I say.

Doris folds her hands in front of her chest, bows her head, and closes her eyes. I do the same. I've never really prayed before, but I suppose it's a good time to start. Doris isn't speaking, so I assume she's saying a silent prayer. I pray to myself, "Dear Lord, thank you for delivering the zombies to me. I'm glad it's finally time for me to fulfill my purpose, and I promise that I won't let you down. I've been told that you do everything for a reason…"

"Amen," I hear Doris say.

"Wait, I'm not done," I say. I continue my silent prayer, "Sorry, Lord, for the interruption. I just have one favor to ask of you: please smite Sarah for stealing my car. Oh, and those two men with the pickup truck that tried to steal my wallet, you can strike them dead too. Amen."

I open my eyes and smile at Doris. "That felt good," I say.

"It's important to pray every day," she says.

"Yeah. So is Howard going to eat with us?" I ask.

"No, dear, he stays in his chair. He has been feeling under the weather, and he's more comfortable over there. I'm sure he'll be all better in a few days."

I'm not so sure about that. I don't want to startle Doris, but she doesn't seem to realize that her husband has been infected. She really shouldn't stay in this house with him. I wonder if she'll consider coming to Jacksonville with me.

The conversation stops while Doris and I dig into our stew. When I'm almost done with my first bowl, Doris asks if I'd like another helping. She does the same after I finish my second bowl. Finally, after three bowls of stew, I am stuffed and exhausted. I let out a big yawn, and Doris suggests that I get some sleep.

"I think I will head to bed," I say. "Thank you again for your hospitality."

"It's my pleasure." Doris smiles and tells me to have sweet dreams. Once I'm inside my room, I lock the door and put a chair under the door handle. After a few moments, I take the chair away. I want to be able to get to Doris quickly if her husband turns into a zombie during the night. She has been so sweet to me, and I can't let her die while I'm safely locked in the guest room. That's the last thought I have before my head hits the pillow.

Jordan's Zombie Booklet Fact Nine

Zombies do feel pain. Some people assume that zombies don't feel anything just because they're dead. That's not true at all. If you shoot a zombie, he or she will feel it just as intensely as a human would.

CHAPTER 10

I wake suddenly to a pitch-black room. I check my watch and see that it's only 3:00 a.m. I hear groaning coming from the living room, so I grab my gun, unlock the guest room door, and slowly tiptoe out of the room. I try to walk quietly down the hallway, but the creaky floors in this old house are making it difficult to move stealthily. I get to the living room and peek over the back of the recliner. Howard is making a noise that sounds like a wheezing snore. He's definitely not a zombie yet. Hopefully, he'll stay alive until the morning. I consider sitting up in the living room to keep an eye on Howard, but I would hate to fall asleep and wake up to find a zombie gnawing on my face.

Quietly, I go back to my room and lock the door. I get in bed, but I can't sleep. I lie awake until 6:00 a.m. and finally fall into a light sleep. I jolt awake at 7:30, and I know that I should get going because I have a long day ahead of me. I walk to the living room to check on Howard, and he seems to be alive.

Doris is humming in the kitchen. Do I smell bacon? I hurry to the bathroom so I can take a quick shower. I put on my clean clothes, stuff my belongings in my backpack, and head for the kitchen.

"Good morning, dear, did you sleep well?" Doris asks.

"Very well, thank you." I look over at Howard, "Good morning. How are you feeling?"

"Oh, he's not much of a talker," Doris answers for her husband. "Would you like some scrambled eggs and bacon?"

"I would love some!" I say. She must have gotten all of these supplies before the invasion. I dig into my breakfast, and my eggs are gone in seconds. I munch on the crispy, smoky bacon, and it's divine (this must be what brains taste like to zombies). I turn to Doris, "Thank you so much for everything. After I finish breakfast, I better head out if I'm going to make it to Jacksonville by the end of the week."

"I'm happy that I could help," Doris smiles at me. "You should take some food and water for your journey." She walks into the kitchen and grabs a box of crackers and two bottles of water. She hands me the rations, and I accept them with a smile.

"Thanks," I say. "This should give me plenty of energy for my walk."

"Are you really planning on walking the rest of the way?" she asks incredulously.

"Yeah, but it's only one hundred thirty miles. I should get there in four days if I try to walk thirty-five miles each day." I am dreading the walk.

"Look, dear, why don't you take Howard's car? You can just return it on your way home."

"I can't take your car, Doris. You might need it."

"Oh, no, I don't drive anymore, and Howard probably won't use the car any time soon," she says. She retrieves the keys from her purse and hands them to me. She must know that her husband won't recover.

"Doris, you are amazing. You are literally saving my life." She beams at me. Doris has been so sweet to me, and I don't feel right about leaving her here alone with her soon-to-be-zombie husband. "Doris, I was just wondering if you would be interested in coming to Jacksonville with me. I'm sure it's safe there," I say as I glance at her slowly decaying husband.

"That's very kind of you, but I'm too old for that kind of travel. Thank you for the offer though."

"I just want to make sure you're safe," I say.

"Don't you worry about me," she says. "Oh, I have something for you. I'll be back in just a minute." She disappears into her bedroom, and comes back out with a book in her hand. "This is for you," she says.

I take the book and read the title out loud: "*Science and Health with Key to the Scriptures.*"

"That should help you on your journey," Doris says with a big smile. She is very pleased with her gift.

"I am grateful for everything you have done for me. You have been so generous, and I wish there was something I could do for you in return."

"You don't need to do a thing," she says. "Helping people is enough for me."

I know what I can do to repay her for her kindness. She'll need a weapon when her husband turns. I grab the gun from my holster where it was hidden under my T-shirt, and I hold the butt of the gun out to her.

"This is for you," I say with a grin.

Doris takes two steps back.

"What are you doing with that?" she asks.

"I want you to have it," I say. I try to hand it to her again, but she won't take it. Oh, I get it. "Don't worry, Doris, I'll be fine without it. I can protect myself, and I'll feel better if you have it."

This doesn't seem to make her feel any better. "I, uh, don't really need a gun," she says.

I beg to differ. It's obvious that she's uncomfortable with guns, so I put the rejected gift back in its holster.

"Take care of yourself, Doris."

She gives me a tight smile. "You too, Jordan. Please be careful."

"I will," I say. I hold up the book, the accepted gift, and smile, "Thanks again. I'll be back by tomorrow at the latest to return your car."

As I walk out of the house, I put the book in my backpack. I still think Doris should have kept the gun. I hope she has time to get away when her husband turns.

Jordan's Zombie Booklet Fact Ten

Zombies hunt in packs. It's not because zombies excel at teamwork, but they are attracted to the same things. For instance, zombies are enticed by the scent of humans. If there is a large group of people, naturally, that is where the zombies will flock.

CHAPTER 11

I walk over to Howard's rusty Grand Marquis in the driveway. It looks like it's about twenty years old, but it's as big as a boat. In any case, driving in an old, beat-up car will be much safer than walking. I can't get over how kind Doris has been to me. I probably owe her my life. I really hope her husband doesn't turn in the next twenty-four hours. If it's safe, I might be able to convince my mom to leave Jacksonville tonight, and she can follow me in her car to Doris's house. I might just be able to convince Doris to come back to Maryland with us.

I really want to avoid highways, but I don't have a map. I should have asked Doris if she could spare one. I check the glove compartment to see if there is anything useful, but it seems to be stuck. I tug on the door for a few seconds until I'm able to yank it open.

A whole pile of maps flies out. Thank you again, Doris. I pick up the one on top and see that it's a Cracker Barrel map. That won't help. I have a mental image of a group of zombies sitting in rocking chairs playing checkers while waiting for their table at Cracker Barrel. I'll take an order of the macaroni and brains, please.

I pick up another map that shows all of Georgia and Florida. Bingo! I map out a route using back roads all the way to Jacksonville.

I start the car, and the engine sputters to life. The gas gauge shows that the tank is about halfway full, which should be enough to get me down to Jacksonville. I look at my watch and see that it's 9:17. If I don't run into too many obstacles, I should make it down to Jacksonville by noon.

The drive is uneventful, and I'm grateful that I don't run into any more zombies. I finally get to my mom's community, and there is no one on the street. I tell myself the empty streets are a good sign. The residents are all probably secure in their homes.

I arrive at my mom's house, and my heart sinks when I see that her front door is wide open. Trying not to panic, I walk up the path to my mom's house and knock on the wide-open front door. Nothing.

"Hello?" I call. "Mom?"

I hear shuffling inside. I put my hand on my gun as the shuffling gets closer. I step over the threshold and see a figure coming around the corner.

Short woman, orange shirt, smiling at me, dark eyes, disheveled hair, smiling at me.

"Jordan?" the figure says. "Is that you?"

"Mom! You're OK! I was so worried about you. Why is your front door open?"

"Oh, I went out to get the paper this morning, and I must have forgotten to close the door behind me."

"I'm so relieved you're OK," I say. "Mom, you need to be more careful," I scold her while closing and locking her front door.

My mom looks at me like she's seeing me for the first time. "Jordan, what are you doing here? How did you get here?"

"I drove most of the way, but I walked for a while too."

"I figured you were coming here. Taylor called me a few days ago. He said he got home from work and found a note saying that you put his family in his fallout shelter. I've been trying to call you."

"Yeah, my phone got stolen. I tried to call you a few days ago, but you weren't picking up your phone." My mom is giving me the evil eye. She uses it when she's furious with me. "Mom, don't be mad. I'm just glad you're OK." A thought occurs to me. "You haven't been bitten, have you?"

She closes her eyes. When she opens them again I can see the anguish in them. Oh no. She has been bitten.

"Mom, don't worry. We just need to find a safe place for you to stay until they find a cure for the infection."

My mom doesn't even look at me. "I'm calling your sister," she says. "Casey will come get you."

"No, Mom, you can't stay here," I plead. She turns her back to me. She's not even listening.

I hear her pick up the phone in the kitchen.

"Casey? Hi, it's your mother," I hear her say. "Yes, fine. Jordan is here. No, everything is OK. Jordan asked if I had been bitten. I know. I'll call the doctor. It'll be fine. OK, I'll see you tomorrow."

She comes back into the room. "Casey is coming to get you. She'll be here tomorrow," she says without meeting my eyes.

"No way! Call her back. It's not safe for her to travel by herself. I barely made it down here alive. The roads are a mess, and the zombies are all over the place."

"Stop!" my mom yells. "Jordan, listen to me. There are no zombies. You need to stop imagining these things. We've been through this, and you promised you would stop doing your zombie drills. You can't keep interrupting your life for a fantasy."

"Mom, you're in shock. You don't have to worry anymore. I'll protect you from the zombies."

"Jordan, look at this," she says. She turns on the television and flips to the news, which features scenes of a kitten fashion show. "Don't you think there would be coverage of the zombie apocalypse on the news?"

"It's dangerous for reporters to be outside right now," I reason.

"Have you stopped taking your medication?" my mom asks.

"Yes," I say sheepishly. "I don't like the way it makes me feel. It wasn't working anyway."

"Why didn't you ask Dr. Emerson for a different kind of medication?"

"I don't trust Dr. Emerson," I say. "He doesn't know anything."

Plus, he smells like tuna fish. What kind of psychiatrist eats tuna fish? You would think he could afford a nice turkey sandwich, or even egg salad. I know I shouldn't use his preference for cheap lunches as an excuse for not trusting him.

"Why don't you trust your doctor?" my mom asks.

"He smells like tuna," I whine. Actually, now that I have said it out loud, it does sound like a legitimate excuse.

"Jordan," my mom says in a tender tone, "Dr. Emerson's job is to help you. You can't keep running around acting like there are zombies taking over the world. You keep getting fired from your jobs because you disappear for days to do your zombie drills, and you need to stop."

"Mom, I'm not just doing this for fun. I'm helping people. You have no idea how many people I saved."

"You saved people? Please tell me you didn't try to shoot anyone this time."

"I only shot a window."

"Jordan!"

"What? I was helping a friend get cigarettes. The window was in the way. If someone wants cigarettes during the zombie apocalypse, then I should be the one to help."

"Zombies don't exist," my mom says in a flat voice, "and they never will."

"That's not true," I say.

"Jordan, I need you to say it. I need you to say the words, 'Zombies aren't real.'"

"I can't."

"Well, then I'm going to have to call Gardner House and tell them to put you on twenty-four-hour watch."

"You can't do that to me."

"Say it," she demands.

I shake my head.

She picks up the phone and starts dialing.

"Zombies aren't real," I mumble.

PART II
(TWO YEARS LATER)

Chapter 12

The stench of tuna in the room is unbearable. I can't even concentrate on what Dr. Emerson is saying. I think he is talking about my progress.

I tried to explain to him that the zombies would be coming, but he doesn't believe me. No one believes me, but it doesn't bother me. I know the truth, and it's going to come in handy very soon.

"Jordan, are you even listening to me?" Dr. Emerson's voice snaps me back to reality. Stinking, tuna-scented reality.

"Yes, I'm listening."

"What did I just say?"

I hate it when people do that. "You were saying that you're proud of me for staying at the same job for over a year."

"That's right. And you have made so much progress. You haven't done any of your zombie drills in more than two years. And you burned all of your zombie books."

I didn't actually burn anything. I just found a better hiding place for my books, but I told Dr. Emerson I burned them. I have continued my zombie drills in secret. But I have to pretend to be normal for my mother. She was really upset when I carried out my last zombie drill in Florida, and I don't like to worry my mother.

Dr. Emerson is still talking, but I can't be bothered to listen. Aren't psychiatrists supposed to listen to their patients? This guy has been babbling for the last five minutes.

"Let's talk about the incident," he says.

"I already told you about it. I tell you about it all the time."

"Sometimes it's different. I want to hear about it today," Dr. Emerson says.

"Fine," I say. "I was nine years old when my dad took me to see *Night of the Living Dead*. It was one of those old movies they play in the park on those big screens. Casey must have been seven, and I think Taylor was twelve at the time. Anyway, I loved the movie, but Casey and Taylor were terrified of the zombies."

"Why weren't you scared of the movie?" Dr. Emerson asks.

"Because I knew I wouldn't have gotten killed by those zombies. I could have protected the people in that farmhouse."

"I see," Dr. Emerson says. "What happened after the movie?"

This is the part I don't like.

"Casey was crying when we got home, and my mom asked what happened. Casey told her that Dad had taken us to see a horror movie. Mom was livid. She sent us all upstairs to go to bed, and I could hear my parents arguing. It went on for a long time."

I pause. I really hate talking about this.

"Then what happened?"

"My dad needed to have the last word. He always did. He said, 'You can't tell me how to raise my kids.' Then I heard him march up the stairs, which surprised me. He knocked on my door and didn't wait for an answer; he just walked into my room. I remember it so clearly. He told me that he was so proud of me for not being scared. I told him that I wasn't afraid of those silly zombies. I said I would have saved every person in that farmhouse, and I could have killed all the zombies. He laughed and wrapped me in a hug." My voice catches in my throat, and I feel a tear roll down my cheek.

"What happened next?"

"He told me he was going out for a little while. He said he would be back soon. He was supposed to take me, Casey, and Taylor miniature golfing the next day. I remember because I was so excited about it." I pause to wipe a tear from my cheek, and I let out an involuntary sob.

"You don't have to continue the story, Jordan."

"I know. It's just that I still blame myself. I feel like my parents wouldn't have gotten in a fight, and my dad wouldn't have gone back out that night, if we hadn't gone to see that movie with him."

"You can't blame yourself, Jordan. It was an accident. We can't control everything that everyone does. You need to stop blaming yourself for your father's death."

"Yeah, I know. But I just wish I could go back and change everything that happened that night. Maybe if I had said something different, he would have stayed."

"We can't change the past. You need to move on and focus on the future."

Dr. Emerson loves talking about the future. His obsession with the future doesn't seem healthy. We should talk about that, but my session is almost up.

"Can I go now?" I ask. "I have to go to work soon."

"Of course. You did very well today, Jordan."

"Thanks," I say. I turn to leave his office.

"Aren't you forgetting something?" Dr. Emerson asks.

He hands me two of the dreaded blue pills. I stopped taking them for a while, so now Dr. Emerson has to watch me while I swallow them. I can feel the pills changing me. I always feel short-tempered after I take them, but Dr. Emerson says they help me think more clearly. I disagree, but what do I know? I swallow the pills, stick my tongue out at Dr. Emerson, and leave the room.

That man is a quack. I try not to think bad thoughts about people, but Dr. Emerson really aggravates me. He says that having bad thoughts is normal. That just doesn't seem right.

I have been abnormally irritable over the past two years, and Dr. Emerson says it's because I'm not "living in my head" anymore. I like living in my head because in there, everyone is kind and innocent. Once you start integrating yourself into the world, you realize that people are nasty, mean creatures. They're worse than zombies. People try to crush your soul and destroy your happiness, but zombies just want to have a little nibble of your brain.

I take a deep breath; I know I need to calm down. I always get riled up after my therapy sessions. As I'm driving to my job at the paint store, I get stuck in a traffic jam and notice a car accident up ahead. I'll never make it to work on time. As I inch forward, my car starts making a strange grinding noise, which is happening more frequently these days. After my car got stolen a couple years ago, I had to spend most of my savings on a beat-up 2002 Corolla with faded white paint. I really hope my car doesn't die while I'm sitting in traffic. I should call my boss and let him know, but I don't feel like getting yelled at. He'll figure out that I'm late when I walk in at 3:15.

I finally arrive at work at 3:23. That car accident was worse than I thought, but I'm grateful my car didn't die. I put on my smock and head to my post. I wave at Debby, the cashier, as I walk past the register. After pushing up her glasses, she waves at me and smiles. Debby is always really sweet to me. I suspect that she is sleeping with the boss, but I don't know for sure. I try to not get involved in workplace drama.

I arrive at my post, but no one is around at the moment. My job is to stand in the middle of the store and ask people if they need help. Everyone needs help. I see couples fighting over paint colors, paintbrush size, paint roller fabric, and pretty much everything paint related. I'd like to inform these people that their wall color doesn't matter because their homes will be invaded by zombies in the near future, and their perfectly painted walls will be splattered with blood.

I try to interrupt an arguing couple to ask if they need help with their paint selection, but I don't get a chance because my evil boss, Jason, strides over.

"Late again?"

Why does he have to ask? I know he knows I'm late. He doesn't give me time to respond.

"Jordan, look, I keep giving you warnings, and you keep screwing up. Why can't you just show up on time like everyone else?"

"There was a car accident, and I couldn't call you because I didn't have my phone with me," I lie.

"This is your last chance, Jordan. No more late arrivals. And you need to work on your attitude."

"I will," I say. "I'm sorry. It won't happen again."

It'll probably happen again.

Jason walks away, and I notice that the arguing couple is gone, but another couple approaches.

"Excuse me," the woman says, "where are your drop cloths?"

"Directly behind you."

"Oh, thanks," she says without looking at me.

They all call me "Excuse me," even though my nametag clearly says "Jordan." It's like people don't actually exist while they're working. Workers are just tools who aren't supposed to have feelings or personalities. You don't become human until your shift is over. Until then, we're all just zombies. We're dead to the world: infected people who need to be avoided, unless, of course, someone needs to know where the paintbrushes are located.

I make it through my five-hour shift, and I leave while Jason is locking up the store. He hates when I leave without clocking out, but I don't feel like talking to him anymore today. I stride out of the store and walk to my car at the far end of the parking lot.

I have exactly thirty minutes to get back to Gardner House before someone starts looking for me. I hate that people have to keep tabs on me now. It makes it very difficult to get away to practice my zombie drills. I have to do everything in secret now. It's not a great way to live, but I know it won't be for long. Once the zombies come, I'll be free.

I get stuck in the aftermath of another car wreck on my drive home. People do not know how to drive. Just stay in your lane and stop when the person in front of you stops. It's not that difficult.

As I pass the scene of the accident, I lean over to take a look. I always look. Everyone looks. There is a woman wedged in the back seat of a beat-up car. She is thrashing her arms, but no one is helping her. A group of police officers is standing nearby, and they seem to be having a serious discussion. They look confused as they glance over their shoulders at the woman in the car. I check to see if Taylor is among them, but he is not, so it's probably his night off.

It only takes me twenty-seven minutes to get back to Gardner House. I rush to the check-in desk on my floor. I'm happy to see that Cyndi is on duty tonight. She is one of the few people that I like here. Cyndi has a sweet, round face, and she always seems to be smiling.

"Hey, honey," Cyndi says, "you made it just in time." She checks my name off her list.

"I wasn't sure if I would make it back. I got stuck behind a car accident. There are some crazy drivers around here."

"Be careful out there," she winks at me and turns back to her computer.

I'm smiling as I head back to my room to get ready for bed. I'm always exhausted after work. I make sure no one is coming before I pull my e-reader from underneath my mattress. Casey used to smuggle in zombie books for me, but ever since e-books were invented, I've been able to read my zombie books without anyone knowing. I still have to hide my e-reader when I'm not in my room because the people who work at Gardner House tend to be nosy.

I start to read my latest treasure, *Deadlocked 6* by A.R. Wise. I've read the first five books in the series, and I can't wait to start number six. They don't want me reading zombie books here, because they think it encourages me to live in a fantasy world. I would be perfectly happy if people would leave me alone to study zombies all day.

I doze off for a while but am awakened by a commotion in the hallway. I get out of bed and open my door as two nurses run past me and disappear around the corner. No one is at the front desk, and it's not like Cyndi to wander off. The phone on the reception desk is ringing.

"Cyndi?" I call out. There's no answer. "Anybody?"

No one seems to be around. Oh well, I'll just let the phone ring. If it's important, they can leave a message. I walk back to my room and shut the door, but I can still hear the phone on the reception desk ringing. That's getting annoying. I think about going out in the hall to pick up the phone, but my own cell phone rings. I'm surprised to see that it's Dr. Emerson's number.

"Hello?" I say.

"Jordan, this is Dr. Emerson. Can you please go get Cyndi for me."

"I don't know where she is. She probably went to use the bathroom."

"Is there anyone else on duty?"

"Not on this floor. They're all gone."

"Damn. Listen, Jordan, you need to get out of there. Get everyone out. You were right all along."

"Of course I was right. About what?"

"The zombies: they're here."

CHAPTER 13

"Well, well, well," I say. "I guess you owe me an apology." My gloating goes unheard, because Dr. Emerson has already hung up. I'm about to snap into action and get ready to evacuate when I realize that this is just a test. Dr. Emerson wants to know if I'm over my zombie obsession, but he's not fooling me.

I turn off my phone and throw it on my bedside table. It's really screwed up that a doctor would do something like that. What stings the most is that he got Cyndi to play along. I should probably find her and tell her she can come out now, but I'm too annoyed. I stomp around my room until I tire myself out. I'm still angry as I crawl back into bed, but I start to feel better once I begin reading *Deadlocked 6* again. I drift off to sleep, feeling much better after getting a dose of my new zombie novel.

* * *

I wake up to a bright morning. I stretch, get out of bed, and glance out the window. It looks like it's going to be a beautiful day, and it's a shame I have to go to work. What a waste of a perfect day. I take a quick shower and pick out my clothes for the day. I pull my box of zombie shirts from the back of my closet. Dr. Emerson doesn't let me wear my zombie T-shirts anymore, but I feel like I've earned one. I'm still mad that he tried to trick me last night. I pull on my favorite blue T-shirt with "This is What a Zombie Looks Like" written on the front. I put on my Baltimore Colts cap and walk to the check-in desk, and there is still no one there. I sign myself out and write a quick note that I've left for work.

I take the elevator down to the first floor and walk out into the sunshine. It's so nice outside that I consider calling in sick and spending the day reading in the park across the street, but I know that Jason is already annoyed with me, and I don't feel like getting yelled at. I trudge to my car and drive to work, arriving at exactly 9:00. Jason is usually here by 8:30, and I expect to see him at the front door glancing at his watch, but he's not there. I get out of my car and walk to the front door. I try to open it, but it's locked. I go around to the other side of the store, and I find that the back entrance is also locked.

Well, look who's late now.

Jason has never been late before, and I can't wait to throw this in his face. I walk around to the front of the store and sit on the steps to wait for Jason. I glance at my watch every few minutes and start to get concerned at 9:20 when Jason still hasn't shown up. Maybe my watch is wrong. I get up and walk to my car so I can check the clock on the dashboard. That's when I see it: the most beautiful sight in the world.

Pale woman, blood on her mouth, shuffling toward me, veins bulging, hole in her cheek, shuffling toward me.

I knew that zombies would shuffle! The one stumbling toward me has disheveled hair, and her skin is so pale it's almost translucent. Her bloodshot eyes are focused on me; she is stalking her prey. I knew this day would come. I take a few steps closer to the zombie, and she is about twenty yards away when I notice something coming around the side of the store. I snap my head to the right and see two zombies moving in my direction. I look to my left, and there is another zombie approaching me, and I realize they're working together.

I can barely contain my excitement. I need to calm down so I can execute my plan. I jump in my car, turn on the engine, and speed off. While leaving the parking lot, I am careful not to hit any of the zombies.

As I pull onto the main road, I see another zombie standing in the middle of the street. I start to count the zombies as I'm driving. By the time I get to Casey's house, I have seen a total of fourteen, including the five sneaky zombies in the parking lot at work. I jump out of my car and run up to Casey's front door. I ring the bell and pound on the door at the same time. I wait for a few moments, but I don't hear anyone inside. I keep knocking for thirty more seconds, and still no one answers. I check behind me and see two zombies shuffling toward me. They're still thirty yards away, so I sprint to my car and close the door before they can get to me. Then I speed off in the direction of my brother's house.

I pull up next to Taylor's house, and I see Greg's car in the driveway. Thank goodness! I'm so glad Casey and Greg came here. I scan the street before getting out of my car. There are four zombies that I see right away, and they're all coming toward me. I sprint from my car to Taylor's front door, and I knock frantically. I hear voices inside, and it sounds like furniture is being moved away from the door. Taylor better hurry up, because these zombies are closing in on me.

I take this opportunity to check out my new friends. They seem to have translucent skin, and their veins are bulging all over their bodies. I didn't think zombies would have such visible veins. I'll have to add that to my zombie fact booklet. Their faces are covered in blood, but their flesh doesn't seem to be rotting yet. The swarm of zombies is only five yards away when the front door swings open and I am pulled inside.

Taylor gives me a hug and doesn't let me go for a minute. "I'm so glad you came here. I kept calling your cell phone, but you weren't picking up. We were about to go out and look for you."

"Of course I came here. It's all part of the plan." I look into the living room and see Veronica sitting in the corner, rocking back and forth. At least she's awake. Casey and Greg are sitting with Taylor's kids. Michael and Owen are now six and nine years old. I have taught them a little about zombies, but I'm not sure they really understand what's going on outside. I notice the television in the corner is switched to the news.

"Do they know what caused this?" I ask.

"No. We've checked all the news stations, but nobody knows how it started," Taylor says.

"I suppose you're happy about this," Greg says, looking at me accusatorily, as if I had manifested the zombie apocalypse. He's wearing a black pinstripe suit, so I assume he was on his way to work this morning. Leave it to him to look stylish during the apocalypse.

"I'm not happy," I say.

"Then why are you smiling?"

Oops.

"Cut it out," Taylor says to Greg. My big brother always tries to defend me, but I can take care of myself.

"I'm not thrilled about this," I say, "but I am ready to get us through this alive."

"Please, Jordan," Greg sneers. "You have no idea what you're doing. You can't possibly think that we're going to listen to you, just because you've read a few zombie books."

"What are you going to do to save us?" I ask Greg. "Are you planning to patent a method for killing the zombies? Or will you try to steal their clients? I don't think that's going to help."

"I will certainly be more helpful than you, psycho."

Greg knows I hate it when he calls me psycho. I respond, "You could entitle your patent, *Method and System for Striking a Zombie to Destroy its Brain and Preparation Thereof*."

"That's enough," Taylor cuts in.

"Patent pending," I mumble.

I walk to the front door to blow off some steam. Those stupid antipsychotic pills are still making me irritable, but now that the zombies are here, I'll be able to stop taking them. I look out the window and see that there are now about ten zombies milling around the street in front of Taylor's house. We need to figure out a plan quickly, so we can get out of here.

"OK everyone," I say. "We need to decide what we're going to do." I see Greg roll his eyes, but he doesn't say anything. "Taylor, how many people can you fit in your fallout shelter?"

"There are four cots, and there is enough food for four people to last at least two months, but all of us can fit in there and survive for about a month."

"Good. Have you called Mom?" I ask.

"We called her last night. She said she's fine, and she gave me strict instructions to not let you go down to Florida."

"Well, that's very sweet, but I'm going," I say.

"Jordan, this is serious. This isn't one of your zombie drills, where the only thing you have to battle is the traffic on I-95 South," Taylor says.

"That's ridiculous. I would never take I-95 South during a zombie drill. You can't take highways during the apocalypse, because they'll be packed with panicky people."

"We can't have you going down there. If anyone goes to get Mom, it should be me," Taylor says.

"You can't go alone," I say.

"I'll be fine on my own."

"You can't stop me from going. If you don't let me go with you, I'll just go to Florida by myself," I say.

"Fine, you can come with me, but you can't leave my sight for a minute," Taylor says.

"Deal," I say.

As long as it makes him feel better, I'll let Taylor think that he's in charge. He calls Mom to tell her to stay inside until we get there. I gesture wildly at him until he hands me the phone.

"Mom, are you OK?" I ask.

"Don't worry about me. I locked all the doors, and I'm staying inside. I know this is awful, but in a weird way, it makes me happy that you're finally getting to live your fantasy."

"Um, thanks. Mom, I need you to listen to me for a minute. Go into your basement and look in the back of the storage room. There is a duffel bag down there. Inside, you'll find a handgun." Taylor scowls at me, and I nod, confirming that I swiped the gun from him. "It's loaded, but you have to take the safety off to fire it. You'll also find two baseball bats in the bag. Keep one upstairs and leave the other in the basement. There is a twelve-pack of bottled water and enough MREs to get you through the week. Taylor and I should get down there by the time your supplies run out."

She tries to protest, but I tell her that she can't stop me from coming to rescue her. I say goodbye and tell her I'll see her soon. I hand the phone back to Taylor, and then I walk over to Casey.

"Jordan, I want you to promise me you'll be careful, OK?" she says, trying to hold back tears.

"I'm always careful," I say. "I've done this several times."

"I know, but this time it's real. I don't know what I'd do if you got hurt."

"You don't have to worry about me. I'll take good care of Taylor, too."

Casey smiles and wraps me in a hug. All of us jump when we hear glass shatter in the living room.

"Everyone, get in the shelter," Taylor orders calmly. I can tell he's trying not to panic. He knows he needs to stay calm for the sake of everyone else.

We rush down the basement stairs and pile into the shelter. It's a bit tight with seven of us in here. The kids look frightened, so I assume they understand what's happening. Or maybe they just sense that the adults are scared. The most terrifying thing for children is to see their parents afraid or out of control. I sit on a cot next to Michael and Owen and ask if they want me to tell them a story.

"Yeah," they say in unison. I see Taylor in the corner packing guns into a duffel bag.

"Once upon a time, there were two little boys named Michael and Owen, who saved the world. Do you know how they saved the world?" I ask them. They both shake their heads. "They protected their mommy from the zombies outside."

"This story is lame," Owen says.

"Fine, I'll tell you a real story. Once upon a more interesting time, the majority of the population was infected by a disease that destroyed people's minds and turned them into monsters that ripped people apart to devour their brains." I'm about to continue, but Michael starts to cry.

"Jordan!" Veronica snaps.

"Yeah?"

"Shut the hell up."

"Got it." I turn back toward Michael and say, "I was just kidding, buddy. That never happened."

"Lame," Owen says.

"Jordan, you ready to go?" Taylor asks.

"Ready," I say. "Do you think we should take everyone with us?"

"I'm not going anywhere," Veronica says. "You all can go on your death trip on your own. The kids and I are staying."

We all look at Casey, who seems to be debating whether or not to go with us.

"I don't think I should go with you. I'd just slow you down," she says.

"I'll stay here and protect you," Greg says to Casey.

"No, you should go with Taylor and Jordan. They'll need you more than I will," she says.

I can tell that Greg is half-relieved and half-annoyed that Casey wants him to leave. He doesn't want to be trapped down here, but he also doesn't want to go out into the zombie-infested streets. I think he'd rather not be anywhere right now.

I wonder if Casey doesn't want Greg to come back. I know that's an awful thing to think, but in one of her drunken monologues, Veronica blurted out that Greg hits Casey. I don't want to believe it's true, but I do find it strange that Casey always has cuts and bruises on her body. She claims she falls down a lot, but I've never seen her do anything remotely clumsy.

Taylor has packed our supplies and tells us it's time to go. We each have a firearm, a bat, and a bag filled with food and water. Taylor seems to think we'll make it down to Jacksonville by tomorrow afternoon. I know it will take closer to four days, but I don't want to dash his hopes. We all get one last round of hugs, and Taylor cautiously opens the door to the fallout shelter.

"Wait," I say. "I forgot to tell you: aim for the head."

Greg rolls his eyes.

"I'm serious," I say. "If you want to kill a zombie, you have to shoot it in the head. But we should try to spare as many as possible in case someone finds a cure."

"OK, Jordan," Taylor says. "We'll try."

We confirm that there are no zombies in the basement, and Taylor quietly closes the shelter door behind us. We walk up the stairs to the first floor, and Taylor fires his gun when he reaches the top. By the time I get to the first floor, I see a zombie on the ground with a hole in her head.

Dead zombie, mouth open, bleeding from the head, blue dress, bloodshot eyes, bleeding from the head.

She is the first dead zombie I have seen. Rest in peace, Zombie Lady. Taylor confirms that there aren't any more of them in the house. He glances out the front window and says he sees about twenty zombies outside. Taylor does have an attached garage, but his cars are blocked in by Greg's shiny, black Mercedes sitting in the driveway. That's one of the basic rules of surviving a zombie invasion: never park in someone's driveway, because the owner of the house will probably want to drive away without having to walk outside and wander into a bunch of zombies. It's Zombie 101. If I had known this was the real deal, I would have brought my zombie survival kit with me. I doubt Taylor will let me go back to Gardner House to get my gear.

I hear Taylor tell Greg, "We'll need to take your car."

"The Mercedes?" he says glumly. "All right."

I can tell that he wants to argue, but there's no point. We either have to take Greg's brand-new Mercedes, or my beat-up Corolla with engine problems.

Taylor swings open the front door and shoots two zombies in the head. My older brother obviously has great aim. Greg has never shot a gun in his life, but I'm sure he'll learn quickly. I have practiced shooting with Taylor at the gun range near his house, but I'm a little rusty. I'm surprised there aren't more brains splattered on the sidewalk. The zombies that were shot just look like regular dead people. This scene looks nothing like the movies I have been studying.

Greg runs outside after Taylor clears a path, and he hits the remote control to unlock the car doors. I'm out last, and I close the front door behind me and run to the car as Taylor and Greg climb in the front seat. I get in and take the seat behind Taylor.

Greg throws the car in reverse and hits two zombies as he backs out of the driveway. The other zombies have enough sense to move out of the way. Greg speeds off down the street and almost hits a mailbox at the end of the block.

"Easy there," I say. Greg ignores me and continues to recklessly weave around the zombies. "Do you want me to drive?" I offer.

"No!" Taylor and Greg say at the same time.

"Jeez, I'm only trying to help," I say.

"Should I take the beltway to I-95 South?" Greg asks.

"Yes," Taylor says.

"No," I counter. "We won't get very far on the highway. Everyone takes the highway to get out of the city during an emergency."

"I'm going to take the highway," Greg says matter-of-factly.

I don't argue. I'll let them see for themselves. The beltway is going to be a nightmare, and I know we won't make it to I-95. I sit back and wait to prove them wrong. They're lucky I have a backup plan.

Chapter 14

We drive two miles to the exit for the beltway, and there are about twenty cars ahead of us trying to get onto the ramp. We need to get out of this mess.

"Hey guys," I say from the back seat, "why don't we just stay on this road? I know a way to get to Mom's house without taking any highways."

"I know," Taylor says, "but your way will take us a lot longer. This way is much more direct. Once this traffic clears up, we'll get moving."

"Fine," I say in resignation. Sometimes people need to learn the hard way that they're wrong.

We finally merge onto the beltway. As we fall in with the mess of cars, I realize that the only reason we were able to get on the beltway is that people are merging over into the emergency lane. Some of the other cars are even starting to drive on the grass. We come to a stop directly behind a huge, yellow pickup truck, and we can't see anything ahead of us.

"Great," Greg says sarcastically, "this is just perfect. Why are these people not moving? Is there an accident up ahead?"

"I'm sure we'll be moving soon," Taylor says.

We sit in the same spot for five minutes, and it starts to dawn on the two men in front that we won't be moving, ever. We're boxed in, and there's nowhere to go. I can't help myself. I have to say something.

"Wouldn't it have been nice if there was a way we could have known this was going to happen? If we had some sort of warning, we might not be in this mess. If only someone had said, 'Hey, it's probably not a good idea to get on the beltway,' it would have saved us so much trouble."

Greg glares at me. I think he wants to hit me, and I'm afraid he might actually take a swing at me, but my big brother cuts in before Greg can do anything.

"You were right," Taylor says to me. He has always been good about admitting when he's wrong. "We should have listened to you. From now on, I'll pay more attention to your plans. Do you have any ideas on how to get us out of here?"

We still haven't moved an inch.

"I do have a plan, but I know you're not going to like it," I say.

"Tell me," Taylor says.

"We're only a couple miles from your house. We should leave Greg's car here and walk back to your place. Then we can take your car to get Mom."

"There is no way we are leaving my car here," Greg says. "This traffic has to let up soon."

"We're not going to be able to drive out of here. If one person runs out of gas or abandons his car, then everyone gets stuck. If we stay here for too long, the zombies will surround us, and then we'll be trapped. The only way to leave will be on foot," I say with urgency in my voice.

"Getting out and walking would be insane," Greg says. "I am not leaving this car. We'll be safe if we stay in the car with the doors locked."

"Haven't you seen a single zombie movie?" I ask. "You can't just sit in an unmoving car. We'll get surrounded by zombies, and then we'll have no way to escape."

"Jordan is right," Taylor says. "We should leave while there are less zombies around."

"*Fewer* zombies," Greg corrects.

"Thank you, Greg. You're being extremely helpful," I say.

"I am not leaving this car," Greg says.

"OK," I say. I turn to Taylor, "While Greg stays here to meet his not-untimely death, you and I should walk back to the house."

Taylor nods and starts to pack up our gear. We won't be able to carry all of the food and water, but we make sure to take all the guns. As we're about to exit the car, a woman rushes past, and a zombie is not far behind. The zombies have already found this bountiful food source.

Taylor has his hand on the door handle. We can't see if there are any threats up ahead because of the massive pickup truck blocking our view. I'm following Taylor's lead.

"Now," Taylor says as he flings open his door. I immediately jump out of the car and scan the area. I see that there are two zombies up ahead, but they're occupied with tearing apart a poor soul. I notice that Greg is still sitting in the car and seems to be debating whether or not to join us.

I tap on his window. "It's all clear now. You can come out." He slowly exits the car and looks like he's going to be sick. Greg isn't accustomed to being in danger. He is the type of person who is always comfortable. If there is something that makes him unhappy, he immediately changes it, usually by throwing money at the problem. The zombie apocalypse is one thing he can't buy his way out of. I do feel sorry for him. He'll eventually adapt to this environment. For now, I'll try to be nice to him.

"Don't worry, Greg," I say. I put my arm around his shoulder, "I'll take care of you." He shrugs me off, but doesn't say anything.

"Hurry up," Taylor says. "They're coming." He points behind us, and we see five zombies shuffling in our direction.

The three of us run away from the approaching zombies, weaving through the rows of cars. I see a few families abandoning their vehicles, but most people are just sitting in their cars, looking terrified. Some are honking their horns. Others are yelling at the unmoving traffic. I feel like I should do something to help them.

"Do you think we should try to get these people out of here?" I ask Taylor.

"There are too many people, and we can't be responsible for everyone," he says.

"I know, but I just thought we could help out a few of these folks while we can."

"We'll try, Jordan, but now we need to focus on getting back to the house to get another car. After we get to Mom and make sure she's OK, then we can start helping people."

"All right," I say. I look mournfully at the people sitting in their cars as we rush away from the calamity on the beltway.

Chapter 15

I see a long line of cars waiting to get on the ramp to the beltway, and I start tapping on their windows. Some people ignore me, but most roll down their windows wanting to know what's up ahead. I tell everyone who will listen that they shouldn't get on the beltway. Some people ask me what they should do; others just thank me and drive off.

I see Taylor and Greg way ahead of me, and I know I should catch up to them, but I keep reaching the last car in line, and then someone else pulls up behind them waiting to get on the beltway. There's no way I'll be able to warn everyone. I wish I had a pen and paper so I could make a sign warning people to stay off the beltway.

"Jordan, come on!" Taylor yells from up ahead. He's waving frantically.

"Fine," I say as I start to jog toward my brother. I hear screams coming from behind me, and I turn around to see six zombies heading toward the cars waiting to get on the beltway. I hope those people have the good sense to drive away. I see a woman in a kiwi-green Ford Focus peel out and hit the group of zombies head on. Two of the zombies are crushed, but the other four surround the car. It looks like the woman is trying to drive away, but she can't seem to. It's hard to drive when you have dead people stuck under your car. I look behind me at Taylor and Greg, and I see my brother shake his head at me. He wants me to let it go, but I can't just leave her in her car to die.

I turn back to the car that's surrounded by zombies. The driver's door flies open, and she sprints away. She's really fast, and I know the zombies will never catch her, but it still surprises me that they aren't even trying to go after her. Then I realize that there is another person sitting in the car, and the driver's door is now wide open. One of the zombies reaches into the car, and I hear a scream come from inside the vehicle.

I don't even look at my brother for permission. I know he'll tell me to leave it, but I'm already running toward the car. I shoot the zombie that's awkwardly trying to climb in the driver's door. I can't get a head shot, so I shoot him in the back. The zombie falls to the ground, and I walk up to him and put a bullet in his head. I take a deep breath. That is the first zombie I have killed, and I didn't realize I would feel so bad about it. As the other three zombies make their way toward me, I shoot them each in the head. Even though I know I have to kill them to protect the woman in the car, I still feel guilty about murdering the zombies. Taylor and Greg finally reach me, and I can tell they're not happy with me.

"I couldn't just leave her there," I say. The woman sitting in the passenger seat is staring at me with wide eyes. I can see that her left arm is bleeding heavily. "Did he bite you?" I ask.

"No, but he scratched me. I don't want to turn into one of those things," she says with a tremor in her voice.

"You're going to be fine. You'll only turn into one of them if you're bitten. It's OK if you get scratched."

"How do you know that?" she asks me.

"Trust me; I've been studying zombies for a long time. You should come with us. We're going to a safe place."

She unlocks the door on her side, and Taylor goes around to help her out of the car. It's obvious that she's in a lot of pain. There are three long scratch marks on her left arm. I look up and see more zombies slowly moving toward us, and this time there are about twenty of them.

We walk as quickly as we can in the direction of Taylor's house. After I'm done reloading my gun, I let the woman lean on me. Hopefully, she can make it to Taylor's house so we can put her in the shelter with Casey, Veronica, and the kids.

"What's your name?" I ask the woman.

"Rebecca," she says.

I can tell it's difficult for her to speak, so I do all the talking. "My name is Jordan. You don't have to worry about anything now. We'll take care of you. My brother lives only two miles from here. If we hurry, we'll get there in less than thirty minutes," I say optimistically.

Greg and Taylor are about ten yards ahead of me, walking on the sidewalk on Old Georgetown Road. The strip malls lining both sides of the street are being looted by the people who usually shop along this road. I see a mob breaking the plate glass window of a Starbucks. A piece of iced lemon pound cake sounds so good right now, but I have to focus on getting Rebecca back to the house safely. Cars continue to zoom by, but nobody stops to help us. Taylor has his gun out, and he's scanning the area in front of us.

Sometimes he turns around and checks to make sure there are no zombies hunting us. Greg is just briskly walking toward Taylor's house. I can tell he can't stand being outside. Well, we're much safer out here than we were sitting in his car.

We have been walking for about twenty minutes, and Rebecca is getting heavy. I look at her face, and she's starting to turn pale. The poor thing looks terrible, and she's having difficulty breathing.

"Hey, guys, I think we need to take a break. Rebecca can barely walk," I say.

"We can't stop walking," Greg says. "We're almost there."

"Well, she can't keep going, and we can't just leave her here. Let's just stop here for a minute," I say.

"One minute," Taylor concedes.

I help Rebecca sit down on a grassy patch next to the sidewalk. I take a step back and stare at her. She immediately crumples over to her right side and starts shivering.

"I think she might be turning into one of them," Taylor whispers in my ear.

"She didn't get bitten," I say. "It would be impossible for her to change into a zombie."

"Maybe she's lying," Greg says. "If you were bitten by a zombie, would you admit to your potential rescuer that you would be changing into a monster in the near future?"

"Yes," I say honestly. "I wouldn't want to be around other people if I knew I would be changing into a zombie, because I would never intentionally put anyone else in danger."

"That's because you're an honest person," Taylor says to me, "but not everyone is like you. There are a lot of dishonest people in the world."

"I don't think she's lying," I say. "See, look, she's getting up. She's fine."

"I don't think she's fine," Taylor says.

Her skin is almost translucent, and her eyes are now bloodshot. Maybe she's just not feeling well. "Rebecca," I say, "do you think you can walk the rest of the way?"

"Uhhhnnnn," she answers.

"I think that's a yes," I say.

"Jordan, she's clearly a zombie," Taylor says.

"But she wasn't bitten. I saw the scratch marks on her arm," I say. Rebecca takes two awkward steps toward us.

"I don't think you have to get bitten to become a zombie. It looks like just a scratch is enough to infect you," Taylor says.

"No, that's just not possible," I say. "Rebecca, you're going to be fine. Do you think you can walk the rest of the way?"

She isn't given time to respond, because Greg puts a bullet right between her eyes.

"Are you crazy?" I scream at Greg.

"Jordan, I don't think you should be calling anyone crazy," Greg says calmly. "You're the one who's mentally imbalanced, so you should watch what you say."

"That's enough," Taylor says. "We need to get moving again."

I'm so upset that I can't even speak. I can't believe that a scratch from a zombie can infect someone. That would mean that everything I know about zombies could be wrong.

Taylor, Greg, and I hurry along in silence. We see a few more zombies in the distance, but they don't bother us. Their food source is still plentiful, and they seem to be taking out the easy targets first.

Chapter 16

We get back to Taylor's street, and what we see ahead of us makes my stomach drop. There are loads of zombies milling around Taylor's house, and it looks like they're even getting inside his house. They must have broken more windows in the living room.

"We need to get everyone out of the shelter," I say. "They're not safe down there."

"Do you really think it's safer outside?" Greg asks. "It's a nightmare out here. The others will be much safer inside."

Taylor looks like he just got an idea. "Jordan is right. We need to go check and see if the shelter is still secure."

Greg agrees, but I can tell he doesn't like our new plan. He just wants to get out of here as quickly as possible. Taylor signals for us to follow him, so we creep toward the house until the first zombie spots us, and then Taylor fires a shot right between its eyes. The rest of the zombies turn toward the three of us.

Taylor and Greg start shooting at the group of zombies. I take a shot at the closest zombie, but I stumble over the curb and accidentally shoot it in the chest. The zombie falls to the ground, clutching its chest. I kick the zombie's foot. "Get up, faker," I say, but the zombie isn't moving. These zombies are smart. They can even play dead, but this one isn't fooling me. I move away from the Juilliard reject and shoot two zombies in the head while backing up toward the house.

We get inside Taylor's front door and manage to close it behind us. Taylor instructs me to start piling furniture in front of the broken window while Greg and Taylor shoot the zombies that are in the house. They kill the zombies quickly and then help me finish stacking the living room furniture in front of the broken windows.

As we reach the top of the basement stairs, we see three zombies pushing on the door of the fallout shelter. They can probably smell the fresh meat on the other side of the door. Taylor puts a bullet in the head of each zombie.

We have to move the zombies' bodies out of the way to get in the door of the shelter, so I volunteer for the job. Taylor knocks on the door with two slow taps and one quick tap, which must be their safety signal. Taylor punches in the code, and the door opens. Casey, Veronica, and the boys are huddled in the corner, looking terrified.

"What are you guys doing back so soon?" Casey asks. "Could you not get to Mom?"

"We got trapped on the beltway, so we had to leave the car there," I say.

"We were boxed in, and we couldn't get out," Taylor explains. "We had to leave the Mercedes and walk back here to get another car. We also had to leave behind some of our food and water because we couldn't carry everything, so we'll have to take a little more of the supply with us."

Veronica glares at Taylor and says, "We barely have enough for the four of us to last two months, and you want to take *more?*"

"We won't take much," Taylor says as he loads some bottles of water into a bag. "We'll just take enough for a week, and hopefully we'll be back by the time we run out of food."

"Don't worry," I say to Veronica, "we'll be back before you know it. We're just going to pick up Mom and help a few people along the way."

"You can't save everyone, Jordan," Taylor warns.

"I can try," I say. "There are a lot of people out there who aren't as fortunate as we are. We have food, water, and weapons, and there are some people out there with nothing."

"I know, but people are going to be different now," Taylor says. "You can't trust everyone. You have to promise me that you won't try to help everyone we come across. I know it's hard for you, but we have to focus on getting Mom back safely. Can you promise me that you won't put the three of us in danger just to help every person we run into?"

"Fine," I say.

It's not fine, but I don't want to let Taylor know what I'm planning. We have to help everyone we possibly can. I look over at Taylor, and he can tell that I'm hatching a plan. He knows me too well. I'm sure he'll come around and see things my way. Once he sees how good it feels to save people, he won't be able to stop. He's a police officer, so he should already know this.

I watch Taylor take something out of his pocket, but I can't see what it is. He walks over and puts his arms around me. I'm touched. It's nice that he appreciates that I want to help people.

Then I feel the cold steel around my wrist. Taylor hands the key to the handcuffs to Casey and tells her not to let me out unless there's an emergency. I can't believe this is happening. My own brother just cuffed me to a water pipe.

Taylor gives Veronica and the boys quick hugs, and, before I know it, Taylor and Greg are gone. I can't speak. I open my mouth to scream, but nothing comes out. I sink to the floor in despair. I can't save the world if I'm handcuffed to a pipe in someone's basement.

Michael comes over and sits next to me. I lean my head against the wall and close my eyes. I can't believe my brother did this to me. The greatest period of my life is going to be wasted in a fallout shelter.

Chapter 17

I wake up with a headache and a stiff back. I must have dozed off, and it takes me a few seconds to figure out where I am. Everyone in the room is asleep. Casey is on a cot in the far corner, and Veronica is sharing a cot with Owen in the other corner. Michael is leaning his head on my shoulder, snoring lightly. I nudge him awake. He looks up at me, confused.

"Hey, buddy," I whisper. "Do you think you could do me a big favor?"

"OK," he says. I can tell he's still mostly asleep.

"Will you go over to Casey and bring me the key from her pocket? It would really help me out a lot."

"Sure," he says.

He gets up and walks over to Casey, then reaches into her pocket and fumbles around for a few seconds. I hold my breath. Michael pulls out the key and turns to me with a grin on his face. "Got it!" he says.

Casey's eyes snap open. "What are you doing?" she asks Michael.

"Jordan asked me to get the key, and I got it." He holds it up to Casey, pleased with himself.

Casey glowers at me as she takes the key back from Michael. "This key is not a toy," she scolds him. "It's very important that you leave this with me, OK?"

"OK," Michael says with shame in his voice. "But Jordan wanted the key." He seems to be choosing his words carefully, "And Jordan is a grown-up too."

"I know Jordan is a grown-up, but your daddy left me in charge, so I make the rules," she says.

"Casey," I plead, "I need to be out there helping people. We have to preserve the human population so we can thrive after we find a cure for the infection."

"Jordan, you can't save the world by yourself. It's better for everyone if you stay down here with us."

"This isn't right…" I start to say before I'm cut off by Veronica.

"Would you two shut up? I'm trying to sleep." Her voice wakes Owen too. Great, now we're all awake.

"What time is it?" I ask Casey.

"Go back to bed, Jordan. There's a cot behind you."

With a great deal of effort, I climb onto the cot. I doubt I'll be able to sleep with my hand cuffed to a pipe. I wonder where Taylor and Greg are right now. They're probably at least in southern Virginia. Maybe they're even in North Carolina. That is the last thought I have before drifting off to sleep.

* * *

I wake up to a loud pounding noise. I roll over and tell an unknown person to knock it off.

"It's the zombies," Casey says. "They're at the door. They got back into the house."

"They're more intelligent than average zombies," I say.

"What is an *average* zombie?" Veronica asks.

"Typically, zombies in movies are slow, and they lack any kind of intelligence. These zombies aren't like that. They're smart, and they hunt in groups. They're going to find a way into this room, and we need to be ready."

Michael hides his head behind his mother. "You need to watch what you say," Veronica says to me. "You're scaring the boys."

"I'm not scared," Owen says with a cocky smile. There's a thunderous crash against the door, and Owen dives behind his mother.

"If you take these cuffs off me, I can get out the door and lead the zombies away. I'm sure they'll follow me out of the house. Then you guys will be safe," I suggest.

"That won't work. You'll just get bitten and turn into a zombie. Then you'll be trying to get back in here to eat our brains," Casey says.

"Please let me out," I beg.

"That's not going to happen," Casey says.

"Will you two knock it off?" Veronica says while she rummages through a small, flowered makeup case.

"What the hell are you doing?" Casey asks her.

"I'm just putting on a little mascara."

"Why? Who are you trying to impress? The zombies don't care what you look like," Casey says.

"When I look good, I feel good," Veronica says.

Casey looks at her in disbelief. "Jordan, did any of the characters in your zombie movies ever apply makeup?" Casey asks. I just shrug, not wanting to get in the middle of their argument. I do remember a scene from the original

111

Jordan's Brains: A Zombie Evolution

Dawn of the Dead where the leading lady puts on full makeup, including fake eyelashes, but I don't bring it up. I know how shallow Veronica is, so I'm not terribly surprised by her behavior.

"Just leave me alone," Veronica says. She turns away from us, and then she puts on some lipstick.

Ridiculous.

The zombies continue to pound on the door, but we realize they're not going to get through. Only a person with the code can get in, so we all begin to relax a little.

"Why don't we play a board game?" Casey suggests.

Michael perks up, but Owen seems annoyed at the idea of playing a board game when there are monsters on the other side of the door. I'm annoyed too. I shouldn't be playing board games; I need to be out there saving the world. I know Casey isn't going to just hand me the key, so I'll have to figure out a way to convince her to let me out. In the meantime, it looks like I'll be playing Monopoly with the kids.

"Dibs on the battleship," I say.

* * *

After two rounds of Monopoly, we're all bored. I haven't really been paying attention to the game, and I'm happy when it's finally over. As we're cleaning up, Michael asks what we should do next. Veronica looks at the stack of board games, and I can tell she doesn't want to play any more games today.

"Um, we could read a book," Casey suggests.

The boys don't look satisfied. I'm sure they miss their television. They should have at least brought video games or something. Taylor hates video games though, and he was the one who stocked the fallout shelter. He only left us with food, water, weapons, and crappy board games. Then he left us here to rot. I have to convince Casey to let me out of here.

"Casey," I say, "you know Dad would want me to be out there helping people."

"That's not true. He would want you to be safe with us in here."

"Dad knew that this would be the most important time in my life. That's why he took me to see *Night of the Living Dead*. He was sending me a message."

"Jordan, that's ridiculous. Dad was an alcoholic, and he was never around. He didn't know who we were half the time," Casey says softly.

"That isn't true. Dad knew my purpose would be to save the world from zombies," I say with less conviction.

"Dad had no idea what he was talking about. If he had known you would turn out like this, he never would have taken us to see that stupid movie."

Ouch.

"He never came back, and it was my fault," I say quietly.

"Dad's death was not your fault. He and Mom got in a fight, he went out drinking, and then he crashed his car. End of story."

"He wanted me to save the world," I say, trying to hold back tears.

Casey comes over to me and puts her arms around me. I just want to be by myself right now, but I don't really have a choice. I let my tears fall until I'm too exhausted to cry anymore. Maybe Casey is right that I'm not supposed to save the world. I'm just a psychopath who can't cope with reality.

* * *

I have given up on getting out of this shelter. The days pass by in a fog. We have been down here for three days, and I can't stand it anymore. We wake up, play board games until the boys start complaining about being bored, and then we sit around and talk about what we should do.

Once in a while, our board games are interrupted by the zombies pounding on the other side of the door. We're about to start a game of Chutes and Ladders when we hear the code being punched into the security door. Either the guys have returned with Mom, or the zombies have figured out how to open the door with the security code.

The door swings open.

"Dad is back!" Michael shouts.

Taylor practically falls into the room with Greg next to him. My brother closes the door behind him, and Veronica screams.

Two zombies, pale skin, shuffling toward us, bloody mouths, bloodshot eyes, shuffling toward us.

Chapter 18

Taylor lunges at Veronica and gets her in his clutches. Her scream is cut short when he sinks his teeth into her throat. I yell at the boys to get under the cot in the far corner. They don't hesitate and are able to slide under before Greg can get to them.

Casey dives at Greg with a baseball bat. He tries to dodge her swing, but Casey is too fast, and she cracks the bat against his forehead. Greg falls to the ground and doesn't have a chance to get up. Casey brings the bat down on his head three more times before she is satisfied. I'll bet she has wanted to do that for a long time.

Casey pulls the key to my freedom from her pocket and tosses it to me. I easily catch the key and unlock the handcuffs. Casey and I move to the corner of the room so we can block the boys from their zombie father. Taylor is oblivious to our presence. He is too busy devouring what is left of his wife. Just like Casey, I'll bet he has wanted to kill his spouse for a long time. It's funny how things work out.

I would try to save Veronica, but I know it's too late to salvage what is left of her mangled body. I hear a cry coming from under the cot, and I realize how selfish I am being. The boys are watching their zombie father murder their mother, so they're probably going to need more therapy than I've ever had. That is, if we make it out of here alive.

Taylor seems to become aware of the presence of more meat in the corner of the room. He lets what is left of Veronica's body fall to the floor. Taylor starts shuffling toward us, so I take the bat from Casey and whack him over the head. He falls to his left knee, but he quickly gets up as I take my second swing. Taylor blocks my swing, and he grabs the end of the bat. He has always been sneaky like that.

Taylor yanks on his end of the bat and pulls me toward him. I instinctively put up my left arm to block him. He grabs my forearm and sinks his teeth into my flesh. I can't quite believe I've been bitten. After all my training and preparation, I get bitten by a zombie within four days of the invasion. This can't be happening.

Casey retrieves the fallen bat and takes a swipe at Taylor's head. This time he falls flat on his back. Casey continues to bash Taylor in the head until she is certain that he won't get up again.

The boys are still hiding under the cot, and I can't imagine how traumatized they must be. They just watched both of their parents get killed. I look over at Casey and see that she has tears streaming down her face. She just killed her husband and her brother in the last two minutes. I'm about to comfort Casey with a hug when she gives me a pained look.

"Your arm is bleeding," she says. We both know what the bite on my arm means.

"Don't worry about me," I say with a fake smile. "You just need to focus on taking care of the boys. They're going to rely on you now. You have proven that you can keep them safe."

"I don't want you to go," Casey says. I can hear the desperation in her voice.

"You're going to be fine. There is enough food and water to keep you guys alive for a long time. We know the shelter door will hold up against the zombies, and the only person who knows the code is now dead." Well, I know the code, but I'm going to make sure I stay away from here. I have no idea how much control I'll have once I become a zombie.

"What are you going to do?" Casey asks.

"First, I'm going to get these bodies out of here. Then, I guess I'll figure it out. I don't know how long I have before I turn. I should probably get out of here soon though."

"Do you want me to shoot you in the head?" Casey offers.

"No! I don't want you to shoot me in the head!"

"Don't be mad. I just thought you wouldn't want to be a zombie."

"It might not be so bad. I'll still be me. Taylor has proven that he still had some of his human memory intact because he remembered the code to get into the shelter. And he seemed to really enjoy killing Veronica."

"True," Casey admits.

"Well, I should get out of here." I turn to the boys, who are still hiding under the cot. "I have to leave now, but Casey is going to take good care of you. You're going to be safe in here. No zombies will be able to get in." The boys don't answer, but I know they hear me.

Casey has tears in her eyes, but I can tell she's trying hard to hold them back. "I'm so proud of you, Casey. I'm not worried about you at all. Just stay in here with the boys, and this will all be over soon."

"I love you, Jordan."

"I know. I love you, too," I say as I head for the door.

The pounding outside has stopped. I cautiously open the door, and I am greeted with a silent, empty room. First, I pull Veronica's body out of the shelter. Casey tries to help me, but I wave her off. I don't want her to touch any infected bodies in case they are still contagious. I drag Taylor's body out next, followed by Greg's bloody carcass. He is one ugly zombie.

I glance at Casey one last time and give her a sad smile. She winks at me through her tears. As I close the door to the shelter behind me, I wonder what kind of zombie I'll be. I suppose I should try to live my death to the fullest. Maybe I'll be a good zombie.

CHAPTER 19

I trudge up the stairs to the first floor. I can't believe my own brother just bit me. I feel like this is all my fault. If I had gone with Taylor and Greg, I could have prevented this from happening. I wish I could have been there to help them. Now I'll never know if my mom is alive. I know I won't make it down to Florida before I turn into a zombie. I don't know where to go. I walk out of my brother's house, and four zombies turn toward me and start shuffling in my direction.

Crap, I forgot that I'm still a potential zombie meal. I stick my hand in my pocket and am relieved to feel my car keys. I dodge the two closest zombies, and I unlock my car door, sliding in before they get to me. I guess it won't matter if I get bitten again, but I'd prefer to avoid another zombie bite.

I turn my key in the ignition, and the car comes to life. I speed down the street and turn left, and then I zoom through a stop sign. I should enjoy my last few minutes of humanity, so I figure it's OK to break a few laws. I aimlessly drive around Taylor's neighborhood until I see a man being dragged into the back of a big, white van up ahead.

I pull up behind the van and turn off my car. I see a woman shutting the back door of the van, so I get out of my car and approach the woman.

Red hair, sweet face, smiling at me, green scrubs, blue eyes, smiling at me.

"Have you been bitten?" the woman asks me.

I can't lie to her. "Yes, I've been bitten."

"Good," she says. "Get in the van."

"I said, I *have* been bitten."

"I heard you. Now get in, quickly. They're coming back."

I look up and see a group of five zombies shuffling toward me, so I rush over to the back of the van. The door swings open, and a large hand pulls me inside.

"How long ago were you bitten?" the man in the driver's seat demands. He is shockingly skinny. If he becomes a zombie, I'll bet he'll only eat small portions of brains at a time. The scrawny man has black hair and huge glasses that are way too big for his face.

"I was bitten about fifteen minutes ago," I admit.

"You still have time," he says.

"What's going on?" I ask, surveying the inside of the van. The woman with the red hair gets in the passenger side. There are bars separating the two people in front from the bite victims in back. I discreetly glance at the two men in back with me. One of them has a serious neck wound, and I doubt he'll be alive much longer. The other man gives me a half-smile as he shrugs his bloody shoulders.

"We're taking bite victims to a safe place," the red-headed woman says.

"Is there a safe place?" I ask.

She doesn't answer.

"How long does it take for a person to turn into a zombie?" I ask.

"Sometimes it only takes thirty minutes, but it can take hours for some people to turn," the redhead says.

"What's your name?" I ask her.

"I'm Anna, and this is Joe," she says, pointing to the skinny man.

"I'm Jordan," I say.

Anna smiles at me, but Joe keeps his eyes on the road.

"I'm Charlie," the man with the less serious injury says to me. He has salt and pepper hair and is wearing a National Marathon T-shirt.

"It's nice to meet you, Charlie," I say. Normally, I would ask him where he lives or what he does for a living, but those things don't seem to matter right now. "So, um, how did you get bitten?" I ask him.

"My wife, Lynne, bit me. I thought she might pull through if I took care of her, so I stayed with her after she was bitten. She turned so quickly that I didn't have time to get out of the room before she attacked me."

"I'm sorry to hear that. If it makes you feel any better, I got bitten by my brother," I say.

He gives me a strange look. I should probably keep quiet for a while. I don't bother asking the other man what happened to him because his neck is bleeding heavily, so he's probably not in a chatty mood.

The van starts to slow down, and I peek out the window and see that we have arrived at a twenty-foot-high guarded gate with razor wire along the top. This place looks safe. I wonder why they're bringing infected people here. I'm starting to get a bad feeling about this.

Chapter 20

The van is waved through the gates, and we drive into a tunnel. This can't be good. Tunnels are never good in zombie movies, where the government invariably has secret underground labs all ready for experimenting on zombies. I don't mention this to the two infected men for fear of alarming them. We pull into an open area, and the two people in front hop out of the van. I try to open the back door, but it's locked.

"Hello?" I call. "Can someone let us out?"

"I don't think they're too concerned about us," Charlie says.

"Then why did they bring us here?" I ask.

"Probably to shoot us before we become a problem," Charlie says.

The man with the neck wound is trying to say something. I can't quite make out his words.

"What did you say?" I ask, getting closer to his face.

"Testing," he groans.

"Testing?" Charlie repeats. "I knew I shouldn't have gotten in this van. I'd rather be shot than experimented on like an animal."

"Maybe it won't be so bad," I say. "They might find a cure, and then we'll all be saved."

Charlie looks skeptical. I think he's about to argue with me, but then he points to the man in the corner. The man with the neck wound starts to shiver, and then he collapses.

"Sir?" I say. "Are you OK?" I give his shoulder a quick tap, but he doesn't stir.

"If this guy wakes up, I don't think we'll have to worry about being someone's science experiment," Charlie says darkly.

I search the back of the van for a weapon. I really wish I had brought a gun with me. When I left Taylor's house, I didn't think I would need a firearm since I knew I would become a zombie soon. Plus, it didn't seem like a good idea to let a zombie walk around with a gun.

The man who collapsed a moment ago starts to move, and Charlie gets behind me. I'm not sure if it's because he believes I can defend him, or if he just wants to put off his death a little while longer. The zombie sets his gaze on me.

I'm in trouble, and I have no way to defend myself. I guess this is it. I was sort of looking forward to being a zombie. I thought it might be an interesting experience.

The zombie tries to stand up, but he bumps his head on the ceiling and falls down. I want to laugh, but it seems inappropriate. I thought these zombies were semi-intelligent. Maybe it takes a while for them to learn.

The zombie gets up again, but this time he crouches. He actually learned his lesson pretty quickly. I raise my fists, ready to defend myself as best I can. The zombie awkwardly lunges at me, but the van door flies open, and an arm pulls me out before he can bite me. Another arm is about to grab Charlie, but the infected man lunges at him, and it's too late to save him. The arm closes the van door. I look up at the person who rescued me, and I see Joe's skinny face staring back at me.

"Aren't you going to help Charlie?" I ask.

"We can't save everyone. That's why we don't learn names," he says. "We're not supposed to get close to the subjects. Now, follow me."

I can hear Charlie screaming from inside the van. "Shouldn't we at least put him out of his misery?" I ask.

"No, he'll be dead soon enough. The other guy will finish him off and have a full stomach, so we won't have to feed him for a while."

"What do you feed the zombies?" I ask. I have so many questions, but this is the first one that comes to mind.

"Meat," Joe says.

"What kind of meat?" I ask.

Before Joe can respond, Anna comes around the corner. "Where are the other two?" she asks.

"One of them turned and ate the other. I could only get this one out," Joe says as he points at me.

"My name is Jordan," I say.

"Well, your new name is Test Subject Twenty-Seven," Joe says as he slaps a plastic bracelet with the number twenty-seven onto my wrist.

"Follow me," Anna says. "We're ready to get you checked in at the lab."

I follow them through another tunnel. They really like tunnels down here. I'm sure they couldn't have built this place in the past few days. This laboratory looks like it has been here for a long time.

"Did you guys know this was coming?" I ask. "I mean, from the looks of this place, it seems like you have been preparing for this invasion for a while."

"No one knew this was coming," Joe says.

"I knew," I say with a grin, "but nobody listened to me."

They both ignore me. Fine, I can play the silent game too.

We walk through two more tunnels and arrive at a huge metal desk. There is a woman ahead of me being held up by two large men. She has chains around her hands and feet. I notice that her left leg is bleeding, and she can barely stand. She looks terrified, and I start to wonder if I should be scared also.

The woman in front of me struggles as one of the men puts a muzzle over her mouth. She tries to scream, but her voice is muffled. I make eye contact with her and give her a reassuring smile. The guards drag her away, and then I get pulled up to the desk.

"Test Subject Twenty-Seven," Joe says to the man behind the desk.

"My name is Jordan," I add, but the man ignores me.

"Why doesn't this one have chains?" the man at the desk asks.

"I went to look for extra chains, but we're all out," Anna says. "Jordan doesn't seem to be an immediate threat."

I am touched that she used my real name.

"At least put a muzzle on it," the man behind the desk says.

"I prefer to be called Test Subject Twenty-Seven," I say snootily.

"I see this one has a sense of humor," the man says. "At exactly what time were you bitten?"

I try to answer as Joe puts a muzzle over my mouth. "I guess about forty-five minutes ago," I manage to say. It's hard to talk with this muzzle over my mouth.

"And how severe is your bite?"

I give him a confused look. "It doesn't feel great," I say.

"On a scale of one to ten, how badly does your bite wound hurt?" he clarifies.

I think for a few seconds, and then I hold up seven fingers.

"I see." The man turns to Anna and says, "You probably have at least an hour. I would get this one to a cell as soon as possible."

Cell?

Joe and Anna each grab one of my arms. I can tell that Joe is trying not to touch my wound.

"You don't have to hold on," I say is a muffled voice. "I'm not going anywhere."

They don't answer. We march down a heavily guarded hallway, and I see a woman in a lab coat talking to two guards up ahead.

Short woman, brown hair, pointing at me, beautiful face, kind eyes, pointing at me.

"That's Dr. Heaney," Anna says. "She's the head doctor here."

I wave to the doctor. She gives me a strange look, and then, after considering, she waves back. We continue down the tunnel in silence until we come to a huge room with about fifty cells. They have metal bars, and it makes this place look a lot like a prison. Only about twenty-five of the cells are occupied. Some are filled with zombies, and others contain people in various states of infection. Some look like they're about to turn, while others appear to be fine.

I'm taking in my surroundings when Anna speaks. "At first, we put all of the infected people in one big room, but the ones who turned first started eating the ones that were in the early stages of infection."

I let out a short laugh. Joe gives me a withering look.

"What? It is kind of funny," I say in a muffled voice.

Joe points at an open cell. "Get in."

Chapter 21

I step into the cell. "Can I have some reading material, please?" I ask nicely.

Anna chuckles until Joe gives her a warning look.

"Sorry," Anna says to me. "I thought you were joking."

"It's OK. I was joking," I say in a muffled voice.

"Do you really want something to read?" she asks.

"No, I'll be fine," I say. "It probably won't be long now." My voice is so muffled that I can't stand it anymore. I remove the muzzle and put it on the bench next to me. I should probably leave it on, but it makes it almost impossible to talk.

"You seem very calm about this," Anna says. She doesn't make me put the muzzle back on.

"It's surreal," I admit. "I've honestly been preparing for this moment for a long time, and I can't quite believe it's actually happening."

"You've been preparing to be infected with a disease that makes you kill and consume other people?" she asks as she closes the cell door.

"No, turning into a zombie wasn't part of the plan. I have always known the world would be invaded by zombies. I just thought I would be saving the world right now, but

I guess if I can help by finding a cure, it will be almost as rewarding," I say with a sad smile.

Dr. Heaney comes up behind Anna and says to her, "You can go now."

"Goodbye, Jordan," Anna says as she turns and walks away.

"Goodbye."

"Do you have any medical conditions?" Dr. Heaney asks me.

"Define medical conditions," I say.

"Did you have any preexisting mental or physical health issues before you were bitten?"

"Define preexisting," I say with a smile.

Dr. Heaney glares at me. "Just tell me if you have any health issues."

"Nope."

"Good. You'll be fully infected soon. Do you have any questions for me before you turn?" Dr. Heaney asks.

"Do you know what caused the infection?" I ask.

"The infection was caused by a contaminated batch of medication that was supposed to treat a blood disorder. Unfortunately, the people who took the medicine experienced horrific side effects that slowed the heartbeat and limited cerebral blood flow."

"So people who took the medicine died and then came back as zombies and started killing people?" I ask.

"No. Everyone is referring to the infected people as 'zombies,' but they're not actually dead. The people who were originally infected lost too much blood flow to their brains, and, for some reason, they started attacking and eating people. We've been studying their brains, and it seems that the infected people have lost the ability to feel empathy. You can't reason with them, and their humanity appears to be gone."

"Wait, so you're telling me that these zombies aren't even dead?"

"That is correct. The infected people are not dead."

"That's ludicrous!"

"You should be happy about this. There is a good chance we'll be able to find a cure. If the infected people were actually dead, there wouldn't be much hope for saving them."

"This zombie invasion is not how I imagined it. I can't believe they're not dead," I say in a huff.

Dr. Heaney is looking at me like I'm completely nuts.

"Sorry," I say. "This is all very shocking. So you still have to destroy the zombies' brains in order to kill them, right?"

"Again, the infected people are not zombies. But no, you don't have to destroy their brains. They are still alive, so if you shoot them in the head, heart, or any vital organs, they will die. We have also found that the infected people can bleed to death, but it takes longer for them to die because their blood is flowing more slowly than usual."

"That doesn't make any sense. You have to destroy their brains. Those are the rules for killing zombies."

"I'm only going to say this one more time: the infected people are not zombies."

This woman obviously doesn't know what she's talking about. "So why are the zombies attacking and eating people?"

"The infection seems to be affecting the victims' behavior, but we haven't figured out why. They're overly aggressive, irrational, and they have cannibalistic tendencies."

Jordan's Brains: A Zombie Evolution

"Eh? Cannibalistic tendencies? That sounds like zombie behavior to me."

"Yes, but I'm just telling you that the infected people aren't dead."

"But if blood isn't flowing to their brains at a normal rate, how are they still alive?"

"The infection keeps their brains and bodies functioning. It's actually quite extraordinary."

"I guess. So you're sure they're not dead?"

"Yes."

"Is the infection global?" I ask.

"No. The infection is currently contained to North America," she answers. I wait for her to elaborate, but she doesn't say anything else.

"So what is this place? Have you been preparing for a zombie invasion for a long time?"

"No. This facility was originally used for experimenting on monkeys."

That explains why these cells are so small.

"What happened to the monkeys?" I ask.

"They're being kept in another part of the facility. The monkeys are almost gone, so we have been rationing them."

"Why are they almost gone? Are they escaping?"

"No. We've been using them to feed the infected people because they don't like to eat meat that's already dead."

"Gross."

Joe comes back in the room and gestures to Dr. Heaney. The doctor starts to walk away. Before disappearing around the corner, Dr. Heaney says to me, "Interesting shirt."

I look down and realize that I'm still wearing my "This is What a Zombie Looks Like" T-shirt. I guess I was destined to be a zombie. I sit down in my tiny cell and take a look at my neighbors. The woman in the cell to my left has already turned. I stick my tongue out at her. "You're not even dead," I say. She is staring at me like I'm a huge piece of chocolate cake. "Sorry, lady. I'm not a meal."

Chapter 22

There are no clocks in the room, but I'm guessing I have been in this cell for at least four hours. Anna and Joe came in a while ago with three more bite victims. All three of them have already turned into zombies. Not me. I'm the last partial human in here. I'm ready to be a zombie now, and I'm getting tired of waiting. I'm starving, but I'm not craving brains. All I want is a huge cheeseburger and a pile of crispy fries. I could really use some water, too.

A short, stocky guard walks past my cell, and I tap on the bars to get his attention. "Excuse me," I say. "Can I have something to eat, please?"

"How long have you been in there?" he asks.

"I think about four hours, maybe five."

"I'll be back in a minute," he says before turning and walking out of the room.

About ten minutes later, the guard returns with a doctor I've never seen before. She is stunningly beautiful with long, black hair and full lips. I look at her big, brown eyes and notice that she's wearing a ton of eye makeup. I'll bet she and Veronica would have gotten along quite well. She shines a bright light in my eyes.

"You said you've been in here four hours?" the doctor asks.

"Yes, but that's just a guess. I lost my watch earlier today," I say. "May I please have some food? I'm really hungry, and my throat is dry."

"I want to take Twenty-Seven to the lab for some testing," she says to the guard. "Get two more guards and bring this subject down to my lab as soon as possible."

"Yes, Dr. Jimenez, right away," the guard says.

"About that food..." I say, but the doctor is already walking away, and the guard has disappeared around the corner.

I don't know why these people are already treating me like a zombie. I haven't turned yet. I still have feelings, and those feelings are mostly of hunger.

The short man returns with two more guards but no food. I'm almost hungry enough to take a bite out of one of the guards, but I'm not that desperate yet. I'll wait to become a zombie before I start devouring people.

"Put these on," the guard says as he slides a pair of handcuffs through the opening in the door.

"Is this really necessary? I'm still human," I say.

"You could turn at any moment, and we can't let you out of your cell without handcuffs."

"Fine," I say. I click the handcuffs onto my wrists. I'm getting sick of handcuffs.

"Put your muzzle back on," the guard says.

I look down at the muzzle on the bench next to me. My cuffed hands struggle to put it on over my mouth. It would have been nice if they asked me to put on the muzzle before making me put on the handcuffs.

The short guard opens my cell, and, once I am out, he attaches chains to my handcuffs. He drags me along a corridor until we get to the lab. One of the other guards makes me lie down on a metal table.

"This is really uncomfortable. Is there a mat you can put under me?" I ask through my muzzle.

"We usually run tests on fully infected people," Dr. Jimenez says as she walks in. "I'm afraid we don't have *comfortable* testing tables." This woman seems to hate me, and I have no idea why. I feel like she should be grateful that I'm willing to be one of her test subjects. "Just relax, Twenty-Seven," she says in a patronizing voice.

This woman scares me. I don't like her, and I certainly don't trust her. She sticks a needle in my arm to draw blood. As it flows from my arm to a bag, I notice that my blood is disturbingly thick. I haven't had my blood drawn in a long time, but I know it's not normally as thick as pudding.

"Does that mean I'll be a zombie soon?" I ask the doctor.

"You're the first person we have studied who is not fully infected. We hope to learn a lot from you. We might be able to stop the infection process before you turn," Dr. Jimenez explains.

As long as I'm helping people, I'll be happy. Doctor Jimenez takes the bag of blood and hands it to one of the guards. "Get this to Dr. Heaney, and tell her to start testing it for any signs of immunity."

"Yes, ma'am," the guard says.

I am about to make a comment on how that wasn't so bad, when Dr. Jimenez takes out another needle and sticks it in my arm. More of my oddly thick blood flows from my body into another bag. How much blood are they going to take?

"Just to let you know," I say to the doctor, "I haven't eaten all day, and it's probably not a good idea to take too much blood. I'm starting to feel faint."

"You'll be fine," the doctor says.

I don't think I will. I'm starting to see stars, and my head feels heavy. The room spins and then goes black.

* * *

I fade in and out of consciousness. I hear people coming into the room, and I recognize Dr. Heaney's voice.

"Can you hear me?" she asks.

I can't speak, but I nod my head. This worsens my headache, so I close my eyes and focus on my breathing.

"Your body seems to be partially resistant to the infection. You are still infected, but it hasn't completely taken over your body. We have never seen this before in a test subject." She pauses for a moment. I peel open my eyes and look at her. She continues, "Before you were infected, were you taking any medication that would affect your brain?"

I nod my head and try to tell her about the drugs that Dr. Emerson made me take, but my mouth won't form the words.

Dr. Heaney starts speaking again, but I can't focus on what she's saying. My head is throbbing, and the pain is overwhelming. I try to lift my head, but the room goes black again.

Chapter 23

I wake up in my tiny cell, feeling nauseous. I'm still hungry, but I'm not thirsty anymore. Maybe they injected me with some fluids after I passed out.

I check out the cell next to me and am happy to see that my zombie neighbor has calmed down considerably. Maybe they tested a wonder drug on her that cured her of annoying her neighbors. I sit up slowly so I can survey the room. I have a few new neighbors, but I'm still the only human in here. I don't see any guards milling around, and there is no sign of the doctors, so it must be the middle of the night. I'll try to get a little sleep so I have some strength tomorrow.

* * *

I've been in here for hours, and I haven't even dozed off. All I can think about is my empty stomach. I can't believe how long this is taking. I suppose I could be immune. In zombie movies, sometimes there is one person who is resistant to the infection. I should probably ask one of the doctors to look into it.

Dr. Jimenez comes into the room and walks right up to my cell with her hands on her hips. She starts talking to me in a language that I don't recognize. It sounds like she's just uttering a bunch of vowel sounds. She raises her voice, but I still can't understand her. She calls a guard over and starts jabbering at him. The guard responds to her in the same gibberish. What are they saying? The doctor is pointing at me, but she's not making eye contact with me. I swear, she is one of the rudest people I have ever met. When I turn into a zombie, I'd like to sink my teeth into her.

I actually kind of want to take a bite of her right now. Her aroma is enticing. Plus, her gibberish talk is starting to get on my nerves. It's obvious they don't want me to understand what they're saying, but they should just leave the room and talk about me behind my back like normal people.

I tap on the bars, trying to get them to keep it down. I gesture to my mouth, indicating that I want something to eat. I wouldn't mind digging into a huge plate of pancakes. However, at the thought of that last word, I abruptly gag. I actually feel the bile rise up in my throat. I've never wanted anything less in my life. I'm starving, but I don't want pancakes. I don't want any food that isn't alive. What I want is a big bite of Dr. Jimenez, and I'd like to eat the guard for dessert.

Holy Hell! I'm an actual zombie. I must admit, this is a lot better than I thought it would be. I assumed that I would feel my body rotting, but it's exactly the opposite. Aside from this nauseous feeling in my stomach, I feel great.

The doctor left the room, but the guard continues to walk past my cell. He keeps pacing back and forth, his delicious aroma teasing my nostrils.

I wish he would go away. I can't concentrate while he's waltzing around the room. All of the other zombies seem to feel the same way because their eyes are also fixed on the walking meat. I keep pulling on the bars, but they won't budge.

Dr. Jimenez comes back into the room and stops in front of my cell. She says a few things to me in her gibberish language then turns to the guard and nods. The guard opens my cell door. I lunge at his throat, but he is too fast. He shoots me in the chest with a Taser gun, which causes me to collapse to the floor. I try to grab the guard, but my limbs aren't cooperating.

The guard puts me on a gurney and secures five thick straps over my body. He rolls me down a long hallway, and I end up in the same lab room as yesterday. There are medical supplies scattered on metal tables along the wall, and I see two other zombies strapped onto gurneys. One looks unconscious, maybe dead. The other is writhing in pain as Dr. Jimenez sticks a needle in his arm.

Dr. Heaney strides into the room, and I try to greet her, but I can't seem to speak. I attempt waving at her, but I can barely move. She ignores me and starts talking to Dr. Jimenez in that same gibberish language, which is really getting on my nerves. I'm not going to tell anyone their secrets. They can trust me. Dr. Heaney comes to my right side and sticks a needle in my arm to draw blood. It actually looks like my blood is thicker than it was yesterday.

Dr. Jimenez walks over to me, says something in gibberish, and sticks a needle in my other arm. The fluid she injects into me is a reddish color, and it burns as it enters my system. I try to break free, but the straps keep me from moving. I start breathing harder; my whole body feels like it's on fire. I never should have gotten in that van. I could be wandering the streets right now, happily eating human brains. Instead, I'm stuck in this hell with these evil doctors. When I was still a human, I thought I would feel some remorse about eating people. Not anymore. I want to tear off Dr. Jimenez's face and eat it as a snack.

Dr. Heaney makes eye contact with me and says something to me in their ridiculous language. I don't respond; I just shake my head slightly. I know they're trying to find a cure, but I don't want to be cured anymore. I just want to find a way out of this place.

Chapter 24

After what seems like hours of torture, a guard rolls me back to my cell. The pain is still so intense that I can barely think straight. As the guard puts me in my cell and removes my handcuffs, I weakly take a swing at his face, but he easily moves out of the way and closes the door. I look at the cell to my right and see that it's empty. I wonder what happened to my zombie neighbor.

Anna and Joe walk into the room, bringing in two soon-to-be-zombies. They deposit the first one in a cell near the door. The second one is put in the cell next to me. The infected person smells tasty, but not nearly as delicious as the non-bitten humans. I would take a bite of a partially infected human if I had to, but it would be like eating broccoli.

Anna stops in front of my cell, so I hold my hand up to the bars. She says something in gibberish and gives me a sad smile. I smile back at her and try to ask her if she'll let me out, but I can't speak through my muzzle. I try to take it off, but my motor skills are subpar right now. The poison they injected into my body is screwing up my ability to move easily. I'm sure they did that on purpose.

I rattle the bars as Anna starts to walk away. She looks back, but doesn't stop walking. I know she can't let me out, but I was holding out hope that she might help me in some way.

I turn my attention to my new neighbor and raise my hand in greeting. She has long, curly hair, and she's wearing a pink dress soaked in blood. She looks terrified, and she has a good reason to be. This woman has no idea what's coming. Within minutes, she starts to breathe heavily. She doesn't look too good, and I think she might be turning. She makes eye contact with me, and I give her a sad smile. I try to comfort her, but my muzzle gets in the way of any reassurance I might be able to offer. I'm not so sure anymore it's the muzzle that's holding back my speech. I think I've completely lost my ability to speak.

The woman in the cell next to me starts to shake a little bit, and her face gets very pale. Her forehead is sweating, and she starts shivering even more violently. She lets out a few muffled screams and then collapses. She doesn't move for a few minutes. I am about to turn my attention elsewhere when the woman's eyes snap open.

Bloodshot eyes, pale skin, moaning loudly, bared teeth, veins bulging, moaning loudly.

I wonder if she realizes that she's a zombie now. I didn't know right away when I turned. I tap on the bars that adjoin our cells, but she doesn't even glance at me. She's probably trying to process all this. I wonder how many zombies are self-aware. Maybe it's just me. I have been trying to communicate with my neighbors, but it seems like there is no verbal communication between zombies.

* * *

I have been taken back to the testing room three times over the past two days. At least, I think it has been two days. I can usually tell when it's nighttime because there are fewer guards, and the night guards always look tired. They probably don't realize that the zombies notice these changes.

I have learned to dread the testing room. The doctors inject me with these horrible, thick liquids. The first one, which was bright red, burned the most. After the first time, I stopped looking at what they were injecting into me. Now I just close my eyes and wait for it to be over. They have taken so much of my blood that I feel weak all the time, and they still haven't fed me, which doesn't help.

While I'm not in the testing room, I just sit in my cell and study the other zombies. The woman in the cell next to me still isn't responding to my taps on the bars. She is probably in shock. Or she might not be interested in me. I suppose all zombies are unique, just like all humans are unique. But I'm sure all the zombies and I have at least one thing in common. I have been starving for the past couple days, and I know the others must be famished as well. I was told there would be meat provided. I have seen no such meat.

This doesn't feel like regular human hunger. It feels more like intense nausea. It's not a severe pain, but I'm aware of it always. The people running this place should think about feeding us. Obviously, they don't have to shove a human into each of our cells, but some kind of meat would be nice. I suppose I could eat animal meat if I had to, but human meat sounds much more appealing.

I wonder if I'll starve to death. That might be what they're trying to do. Maybe they want to figure out if it's possible for zombies to die from starvation.

Jordan's Brains: A Zombie Evolution

I perk up when I see Anna and Joe enter the room. I wave at them, but they ignore me. They are concentrating on keeping an almost-zombie under control.

Giant man, pale skin, thrashing his arms, scared eyes, bloody clothes, thrashing his arms.

I'm pretty sure this man is about to turn into a zombie. His skin is turning pale, and he is shivering all over. I notice that he's wearing a Redskins sweatshirt and sweatpants set. Stylish. Anna, Joe, and a tall, skinny guard who I've never seen before are rushing to get this man into a cell, but I know it's too late when the man collapses. They only have a few seconds to get him locked in a cell before he wakes up as a zombie. The guard picks up his legs as Anna and Joe grab his upper body and drag him toward a cell across the aisle from me.

The man is almost in the cell when his eyes snap open. He grabs Anna and is able to move his muzzle enough to dig his teeth into her shoulder. The guard shoots the zombie in the arm, which causes the infected Redskins fan to drop Anna and turn his attention to the guard. He fires again and hits the giant zombie in the shoulder. As the guard gets ready to fire a third time, the zombie grabs him and pushes him up against my cell.

I lunge at the guard, and I'm able to grab the keys from his belt before the giant zombie lets him fall to the ground. I look at the keys in my hand. I have watched the guards use the passkeys, and I know all I have to do is swipe the key in front of my lock to open the door. The question is, do I want to join in the fight outside my cell?

Yes, I believe I do.

Chapter 25

I unlock the door and step out of my cell. The first thing I do is put Anna in an empty cell, because she won't be safe after I complete the second part of my plan. I don't know where Joe went, but I assume he ran off to get help. After Anna is safely in her cell, I notice that the giant zombie is happily munching on the guard whose keys I borrowed. I'll thank the giant zombie for my freedom later.

I know I have to move quickly because I'm sure there are more guards on the way. I hold the passkey up to my neighbor's cell. My hands aren't as coordinated as they used to be, but they're still functioning. The door swings open, and my zombie neighbor emerges and walks directly over to the dead guard and joins in the feast. I wish I could join her, but that will have to wait.

I quickly move down my row of cells, letting the zombies pour forth. I get to the end of the row, and I'm about to open the cell of a man who is hovering in the corner. I realize just in time that he hasn't turned yet. He is staring at me, terrified. I leave him in his cell for his own safety.

I move clumsily to the next row of cells, and I start freeing the next wave of zombies. Several more guards charge into the room and fire their guns at the zombies feasting on the fallen guard. The remains of the first guard are almost gone. Maybe the guards wouldn't be in this situation if they had just given us a snack once in a while.

The zombies turn their attention away from their feast to the more pressing issue of the living guards. By now, there are twenty free zombies and only five guards; even with their guns, they don't stand a chance. I have almost reached the end of the second row and am about to make my way around to the last row of cells when one of the guards realizes what I'm doing.

She aims her gun at my head. I duck, as if that's going to help. I'm waiting for a bullet to shatter my skull, when the giant zombie tears into the guard's face. She screams, and her weapon falls to the ground. Now I owe the giant zombie two favors.

I cross over to the last row of cells. I have eleven more zombies to free, and then I'll try to find a way out of here. After more guards rush into the room, I count eight living guards. Once I free the last prisoner, there will be thirty-two zombies in the room. This isn't a fair fight. The guards don't seem to have great aim, and I don't think they are trained soldiers. Before the infection broke out, they were probably nurses and lab technicians and were never trained to deal with this type of situation. I feel a little sorry for the guards. Nevertheless, I shuffle over to join the fight after freeing the last zombie.

The zombies have the guards completely surrounded. Even though they smell delicious, I don't want to kill any of them. When I was trapped in my cell, it was easy to fantasize about tearing into the guards' flesh, but now that I'm being presented with the opportunity, I don't think I can actually hurt anyone. I turn away from the bloodbath and decide to stand off to the side until all the guards are dead. Once the screaming subsides, I turn back around and see that all the guards have been killed, and their remains are being devoured quickly. I snatch a slender, hairless forearm from the pile of meat. I don't know who this arm belonged to, but I silently thank her for her sacrifice.

I sink my teeth into the sweet flesh. This is delicious. I smack my lips and go for seconds. I always thought that zombies only ate human brains, but this flesh is scrumptious. I guess most of my zombie fact booklet is inaccurate. I blame the movies.

I don't feel as bad as I thought I would about eating these people. After all, they were holding us captive and torturing us. I dig out part of a torso and greedily slurp the meat. This is just too good. After I finish another chunk of meat, I contemplate digging in for more, but I decide that I need to focus on getting out of here. I still have the key to the cells, and I wonder if it opens the outer doors as well.

I shuffle away from the group and try using the key on the door to the hallway. It doesn't work, so I stumble back toward the group, hoping to retrieve the key to the outside from the guards' remains. As I'm making my way back to the group, I hear someone tapping on a cell door. I look up and see Anna holding a keycard up to the door.

I look back at the other zombies, and they are still occupied with feasting on the guards. I wonder if I can get Anna out of here safely. I'll have to try. I open the cell door, and Anna tosses the key out to me and closes the door again. I look at the exit and then back at her. She looks at the group of more than thirty zombies and shrugs her shoulders. I shake my head; I'm getting her out of here. If she stays, the doctors will test their evil drugs on her once she becomes a zombie, and I can't let that happen.

I open her cell door again and pull her out. Now that she's out in the open, she knows we have to make a quick getaway before the feasting zombies notice her. She takes the key back from me and runs for the door as I shuffle after her. I hear the man in the end cell frantically banging on his door. I quickly unlock the door to his cell and pull him out. He jumps at my touch. I hold up my hands as if to say, "I'm not going to hurt you." I kind of want to sink my teeth into his slowly decaying flesh, but I won't because I'm a decent zombie. Plus, I just ate.

Anna opens the door to the hallway and wildly gestures at us. She's talking in that gibberish language, which I now realize is how all humans sound to zombies. I look back at the group of zombies, and a few have broken away from the group to come after us. Anna runs down the hallway, and the man and I follow her out the door.

We turn right and rush down a long corridor with dark walls and minimal lighting. The two humans are much faster than I am, but I'm trying to keep up. I look behind me and see a group of five zombies stumbling after us. I'll be OK as long as I shuffle faster than them. I know it's not me they're after, but I would much rather stay ahead of them.

Anna leads us to the end of another corridor and swipes her key card against a door. The door opens and I'm temporarily blinded by a bright light. I haven't seen the sun in days. Anna takes a quick look around and gestures for us to follow her. We make our way along the outside of the brick building where we were held captive. I see a heavily guarded fence ahead of us, and I know we can't get past them. If we stop here, the zombies will catch us; if we move forward, the guards will shoot us.

Anna starts to sprint back toward the zombies that are shuffling in our direction. I have no idea what she's up to. There are more and more zombies pouring out of the exit. Part of me is glad they followed us. I want them to be free so they don't have to be tortured any more, but I don't want them to get Anna. She is, after all, the one who led us to freedom. Well, almost; we're not exactly free yet.

I watch as Anna lures the zombies toward the exit at the other end of the building. The guards at the first entrance catch sight of the zombies and fire into the crowd. I look behind me and see the partially infected man who I let out of his cell get torn apart by three zombies. Sorry, buddy. Anna gets to the second entrance and opens the gate with her passkey.

The guards at the second entrance shoot at Anna, and I can't get to her in time. One guard shoots her right in the stomach. She falls hard, and the zombies start to close in on her. Most of them are shuffling out the gate, but four of them surround Anna. I shove one of them aside and take a swing. I barely make contact with the zombie because I'm clumsy and off-balance. One of the guards saves me a little trouble and shoots my opponent in the head. The same guard then aims his gun at me. I dive over Anna, and the guard misses me by inches. I am protecting Anna from bullets and zombies, and I know I need to get her out of here right now if I'm going to keep her alive.

Fortunately, a second wave of zombies emerges from the brick building, and the guards start firing at the others. I look sternly at the zombies surrounding Anna, but they're not backing down. A guard takes out another one, so I'm only contending with two zombies now. With great effort, I throw Anna over my shoulder and make my way toward the main exit. The other two zombies are shuffling next to me, gnawing on Anna's arms. She doesn't scream, so I think she might be unconscious.

I start to stumble under her weight. I don't know how much longer I can carry her. I am freed from my burden when the giant zombie comes up behind me and takes Anna from my arms. Now I guess I owe him three favors.

No, wait, he's eating Anna's face. I know that she is beyond saving, so I shuffle away from the laboratory. I look back and see three zombies chewing on Anna. I feel my heart break a little. Not for Anna. For me. She is probably better off dead, but I would have enjoyed her as a zombie companion.

A few bullets come within inches of me as I'm making my escape, but none of them make contact. I come to a nearby wooded area and know that I'm safe. I make my way into the forest to look for shelter. The sun will be setting in a few hours, and I don't want to be out in the open when it gets dark. I assume the people from the lab will come looking for me. I'm still hungry, but I'll wait until tomorrow to look for food. Tonight, I'm going to rest so I'll be ready to start my new life as a free zombie tomorrow.

Chapter 26

Finding food is harder than I thought it would be. I have been shuffling for hours, and I haven't come across a single living person. I run into two zombies, but I don't think they are from the lab. I decide to follow them for a while. They don't seem to mind my presence, but I realize they're shuffling in circles. I get bored and decide to go off on my own.

I prefer to be by myself. I have to think of this as an adventure. I would feel a lot better if I could just find some food. I come across a tiny log cabin in the woods, but it's deserted. I take about an hour to scour the area, but I don't find anyone. I wonder how many humans are left. Hopefully, there will be enough food to go around.

Then I think about Casey and the boys and wonder how they're holding up. They should have enough food for at least two months. I hate the idea of them leaving the fallout shelter to find food. I consider going to Taylor's house to check on them, but I don't want to lead any zombies back there. It's better if I just stay away from my family.

I feel like I need a plan or a purpose or something. I mean, searching for human flesh is fine, but I want to do something creative or useful with my time. Maybe I can find some more zombies so we can band together and act out the scenes from my favorite movies. What would the zombies in *Night of the Living Dead* do? I could find a farmhouse to surround. Or, I could remake a scene from *Shaun of the Dead* by surrounding a bar. That would be fun, but I lack the horde of zombies for the *surrounding* portion of my plan.

I stumble around the woods, trying to find the giant zombie from the lab. Even though he devoured Anna, he would be a huge asset to my cast. I mean my pack. Yes, pack sounds better.

I don't run into the giant zombie, but I do find two zombies that seem happy to follow me around. They're scrawny, but they'll do for now. The three of us come across a large, white farmhouse with red shutters. Even though the house looks deserted, I'm very excited about the prospect of acting out my favorite *Night of the Living Dead* scenes.

Of course, when I was a kid, I was rooting for the humans. I'm sorry, but it's much more fun to be a zombie. My two new friends follow me as I start circling the farmhouse. I think I smell human flesh, but it must be my imagination. The lights are out, and I can't see any movement in the house. I know there's no one inside, but it's kind of thrilling to reenact scenes from the movie that started it all.

After circling the farmhouse three times, I start getting bored. OK, this movie idea was stupid. I just want to find some food. When I'm about to give up on my movie plan, I hear a crashing noise come from inside the house. I shuffle over to the front of the house with the two zombies following me.

I pound on the front door, and my two friends follow my lead. I wonder how many people are inside. I hope there will be enough meat to go around. The door won't budge, so the three of us make our way around to the back of the house and find a sliding glass door. I bang my fists on the glass, and the other two zombies join me. After pounding for several minutes, I realize that the glass isn't going to shatter like it does in the movies. Those zombie movies are really throwing me off.

I spot a rock nearby that I'm guessing weighs about ten pounds. I grab the rock, and, with much effort, I hurl it at the door. The glass shatters, and we push our way inside the house. As the three of us shuffle into the house, we hear a door slam upstairs. Jackpot! I slowly climb the stairs with the two zombies right behind me. As I'm about to get to the top, I hear a gunshot. I really don't want to get shot, so I let the other two zombies go ahead of me.

They approach the closed door, and, of course, it's locked. The three of us throw our weight against the door several times, and it finally swings open. I stumble into the room and see a man lying on the bed.

Gun in mouth, tear-filled eyes, bleeding from the head, unshaven face, mouth agape, bleeding from the head.

It's better this way. Now we don't have to worry about killing this guy. We can just enjoy the feast. The three of us eat every scrap of meat, and I finally feel satisfied. It's getting dark outside, so I decide to stay in the cabin for the night.

My two zombie friends follow me around the house, mimicking my every move. It appears they have chosen me as their leader. For the entire night, I teach them defensive moves, like putting their hands up to protect their heads. I also teach them to block weapons and dodge bullets. I think I actually enjoy being a zombie. My zombie friends and I aren't able to communicate verbally, but they understand my hand signals. If I hold up my hand, they stop. If I wave my hand forward, they follow me. I have a feeling we will be a good team.

I feel some remorse about the man that we ate earlier this evening. Technically, we didn't kill him, but I know he killed himself because we were in his house. Is it still considered murder if you're a zombie? Maybe I should just think of it as grocery shopping; that sounds much more civilized.

I try to think of ways to survive the infection without actually killing anybody. I'm sure we'll be able to scrounge up some previously deceased food. We'll just have to learn to be sneaky.

After working with the other two zombies for most of the night, we rest for a while and then leave at dawn. I figure it's much safer to travel during the daytime because we will be able to spot any attackers before they can get to us. We can't move quickly, so we need to stay close to the woods so we'll always have a place to hide.

I'm a little hungry again, but I'm not starving like I was yesterday. I guess zombies have to eat every day too. I hope we run into more food sometime today.

As we shuffle through the woods, I spot some movement up ahead. We start to stumble in the direction of the disturbance, when I notice that our soon-to-be-meal is on four legs. We get within ten yards of the animal, and it looks like a mutt. He's a scrawny dog with black, matted hair, and I think he might be part Labrador.

The zombie to my right lunges at the mutt, but I block him so he can't get the dog. I have seen too many movies where an innocent dog gets killed, and I can't stand it. I have to keep this dog alive. He smells fairly tasty (not as good as human meat, but still edible). I turn to the two zombies and hold up both hands, signaling for them to stop, but they won't leave the dog alone. They keep lunging at my new canine friend. I slowly back up while blocking my four-legged friend from danger, but the zombies are determined to eat him for lunch. I try to shove them away, but they won't stop going after the dog.

I gesture wildly at the dog, trying to get him to run away. The zombies are getting frustrated, and they're very close to getting their hands on him. I won't let any dogs die in my story. I pick up a stick and heave it as hard as I can in the opposite direction. It only goes about five yards, but the dog goes after it. Good, now he can get away from us monsters.

No! Why is he bringing the stick back? Doesn't this dumb dog know anything about danger? Didn't his mother teach him not to play with zombies? I take the stick from his mouth and throw it harder this time. It doesn't go much farther than five yards.

An idea pops in my head that might save the dog. It's a risk, but I think it'll work. I step back and let the two zombies go after the dog. They aren't very fast, so he has plenty of time to get away. The zombies stumble toward the dog, and he bolts in the other direction and disappears into the forest. Good luck, my friend.

CHAPTER 27

My pack of three continues along the edge of the woods of what I believe is rural Maryland. I can't read any of the street signs we've passed, but I don't think I'm too far from home. We're close to a main road, so we'll be able to spot any attackers (or meals). It's still springtime, so there is plenty of foliage to keep us concealed. My zombie friends seem to have forgiven me for not letting them eat that dog for lunch. Either they forgive easily, or they forget quickly.

My two friends and I come across a pack of four zombies emerging from the woods. I wave at them, trying to look friendly, but they ignore me. I quickly determine which zombie is the leader. She is trudging ahead of the other three.

Short zombie, greasy hair, shuffling away from me, dead eyes, blood on her mouth, shuffling away from me.

I try to get her attention, but she is actively ignoring me. I know she sees me. My two zombie friends and I continue to shuffle along with the other group. I'm determined to expand my pack because we'll have a better chance of surviving if there are more of us.

The new zombies don't seem to mind that we have joined their pack. The lead zombie has pulled ahead of me, making it clear that she is in charge of this pack. That's fine with me. I'll let her think she is in charge. The four new zombies have obviously eaten recently. They are covered in fresh blood, which is a sign that they know how to hunt, so I figure it will be beneficial to stick with them.

We hear a commotion up ahead, and the lead zombie puts her hand up, signaling for us to stop. That's *my* move. I guess I'm not the only zombie with intelligence. I thought that I was an anomaly because of my special brain.

We stop and duck behind a huge tree. The lead zombie sticks her head out to survey the scene up ahead. I poke my head out too, and she gestures for me to get back behind the tree. I've never been good at following directions, so I come out from behind the tree and start to shuffle toward the action. I stop when I feel something hit the back of my leg. I look behind me in disbelief. The lead zombie threw a rock at me. Rude!

I turn back toward the commotion. I don't care if there is danger ahead; I can't go back to the rock-thrower. Then she'll think she has won. I am about twenty yards from the scene, and I notice that there is a pack of zombies kneeling in front of something. I walk right up to the group, but they don't seem to notice me, so I push my way through the crowd and see two dead bodies being devoured quickly. I'm glad I came over when I did because this meat isn't going to last long. I snatch up an arm and another unidentifiable piece of meat then separate from the crowd and shuffle back to my zombie pack.

As I get closer to the lead zombie, I realize that she's pissed. She is glaring at me with her bloodshot eyes. I shrug my shoulders and give her an innocent look. I hold up the arm and extra meat with a grin on my satisfied face. I know the lead zombie is angry at me, but I redeem myself by tearing the meat into seven small pieces. Everybody gets a fair share, even though I risked my life to get this meat. The lead zombie nods her head at me in approval. I think that means she's going to let me stay with the pack.

The meat is delicious and gone too quickly. We're going to need to find more food soon. I look at the lead zombie for directions, and she gestures at us to follow her deeper into the woods. I have accepted her as my leader. I assume she has killed many people, so I'll just think of her as my meal ticket.

* * *

The first creature my expanded pack comes upon is not human. Well, I'll be damned; I had no idea there were black bears in rural Maryland. The lead zombie gestures for us to spread out so we can surround and ambush the bear.

Nope. No, ma'am. Bad idea.

I try to shuffle away from the bear, but the leader grabs my arm and glares at me. Good Lord, she's frightening. Fine! We'll do it her way. Let's fight a bear. No big deal.

Somehow, we manage to surround the bear without alerting it to our presence. It notices us as we start to close in. The bear stands on its hind legs and snarls. It crushes one zombie that tries to attack it from the front as three other zombies jump on it from behind. The bear tears into the first zombie's flesh as the others latch onto its back. I'm standing back, not sure what to do. The leader gestures for me to join the fight. The bear is on the ground, struggling to get to its feet, but my leader stops it by sinking her teeth into its throat and tearing out a huge chunk of flesh.

I guess it's safe to join in now. I start eating once I know for sure the bear isn't going to get up. This meat is surprisingly good. It's not as good as human meat, but it's still satisfying. Maybe I can survive on animal meat for the rest of my time as a zombie. That would be ideal. But I will *not* be eating any dogs.

After eating every scrap of meat, the six remaining pack members decide to move on. It's dark now, and we'll probably want to find a place to take a break. Even though zombies don't sleep, we still like to rest. Shuffling all day is hard work, and we need to give our infected bodies some time to recuperate.

The lead zombie directs us to a clearing in the woods with plenty of space to stretch out. There are several trees nearby if we need a place to hide. The lead zombie sits down and leans against a tree, and I follow her example.

I don't close my eyes, but I am able to mentally drift off. I think about Casey and the boys. I don't know how long it has been since I left them. It's difficult to keep track of time when you're a zombie. That's probably because time doesn't matter anymore. I won't ever have to go to work again, and, happily, I won't have to go to therapy anymore. It's nice to not have to worry about being late. I suppose being a zombie has its perks.

Chapter 28

At dawn, the lead zombie is on her feet and gesturing for us to get up. The rest of us stand up and start to follow her back to the road. A few cars drive by our pack, and the lead zombie signals for us to duck behind trees while they pass us. After we come out from behind the trees, we come upon a broken-down car, and the lead zombie signals for us to follow her toward the vehicle.

One of the windows in the back seat is broken, but there is no sign of blood. The humans must have gotten away. We hear a crashing noise up ahead, followed by the sound of a woman screaming.

The lead zombie starts to move in the direction of the screams with the five of us following behind her. I don't see anything for a while, then out of nowhere two humans come rushing toward us, but they don't see us yet. Suddenly, the man snaps his head around and stops short. The woman looks up to see why and screams when she spots us. Another large pack of zombies is chasing them from the other direction. Our pack spreads out as the other pack reaches us, and we have the humans surrounded.

The man tries to push through the crowd of zombies, but my leader latches onto him and bites his shoulder. The leader from the other group pounces on the woman, and the feeding frenzy begins. I want to wait until the humans are dead, but the meat smells too good, and I can't stop myself. The woman is still screaming as I sink my teeth into her leg.

In order to enjoy my meal, I have to justify my actions. Technically, I didn't kill anybody. These people were going to die anyway. Sure, I didn't try to save them, but I don't think I would have been able to help this couple. I would have just delayed their demise, so I did the right thing by helping them die as quickly as possible.

After we have cleaned all the meat off the bones, the ten zombies get up and survey each other. We are a sad-looking bunch. Each of us is covered in blood; our clothes are torn and soiled with scraps of human tissue. I suppose this is what a successful zombie pack looks like.

The leader from the other group stands in front of our leader. It looks like they're communicating in some way. Maybe they're figuring out who will be president and who will be vice president of the newly expanded pack. The two leaders break away from the group and stop in a field about twenty yards away from the rest of us. We watch as the two leaders face each other.

I shouldn't be surprised by what happens next, but I can't quite believe my eyes as I watch the two lead zombies start fighting. I assume they're planning on fighting to the death to determine the new leader. This is the most bizarre fight I have ever witnessed. My leader tries to punch the male leader's throat, but he dodges her blow. He tries to kick her, but he misses and ends up falling to the ground. This could take a while. I find it strange that none of the other zombies are joining in the fight. I glance at the rest of the pack, and they all have their eyes on the battle. I suppose I should be paying attention too.

My leader punches the other zombie directly in his jaw, and he answers her by kicking her in the stomach. She folds over and the other zombie leader takes advantage of her bent-over position by kneeing her in the head. She falls down, but she's not done fighting. She grabs the male leader's foot as he tries to stomp on her head. She twists his foot so it's facing backward. The male zombie falls down, and the female crawls over to him then grabs his head and twists until his neck breaks. Lesson learned. I will never start a fight with my leader, because she can kill a zombie with her bare hands.

The leader of this new nine-zombie pack makes her way over to us. She drags the recently deceased leader's body over to the rest of the group and limps up to the three new zombies while holding the dead body up to them. Each of the new zombies touches the cheek of their former leader, followed by the cheek of their new leader. This must be some weird zombie ritual. After each of the three zombies has touched all of the required cheeks, the reigning leader tosses the dead body aside.

This zombie ritual is really creepy. I've never seen anything like this in any of the zombie movies I've watched. I wonder why my leader never made me touch her cheek. Maybe I was supposed to do it, but I didn't realize it at the time. That's probably why she didn't challenge me to a death match. She must have known that I was ignorant about zombie traditions, so she just absorbed my small pack into hers.

Jordan's Brains: A Zombie Evolution

I glance at the dead body and wonder where zombies go after they die. Do they go to hell with the rest of the evil human population? Or is there a special hell for zombies? I wonder if it's possible for zombies to make it into heaven, if they are on their best behavior. I'm guessing not, but there might be a chance. I'd really rather not find out.

Chapter 29

The three new zombies don't seem to be mourning the loss of their dead leader. I'm relieved that they're not holding a grudge against us, because that would make things really awkward. The nine of us walk along the edge of the woods for the rest of the day, but we don't hunt anymore. We've had enough excitement for one day. As night falls, we make our way back into the woods to find a place to settle down for the evening.

We spend the next few days scouring the woods for food, but we haven't seen a single human in three days, and the whole pack is starving and frustrated. I think the remaining humans have gotten wise and are staying inside. It looks like we'll have to start breaking down doors. At least there are nine of us now, which should make it easier to break into people's houses.

We come across a two-story brick home with blue shutters and a huge garden that is surprisingly still blooming. There are no lights on in the house, but I can smell the flesh inside. My mouth waters as we approach. I'm not thinking about getting into zombie heaven right now. All I care about is filling my stomach.

The leader gestures for four of us to go around back, so I take charge and lead the first group into the backyard. We find a sliding glass door with the shades drawn. I look around for something to break the glass, but I don't see anything that could shatter a window. I start pounding on the glass with my fists, and the three other zombies follow my lead. We pound and pound, but nothing happens. My hands are starting to throb, and I don't have a backup plan. I can't go around front and admit defeat to my leader.

That's when I hear glass shatter, but it isn't our glass door that breaks. The noise came from the front of the house. I peek around the corner and see that my leader has shattered one of the windows in front. I look up and notice a rifle pointed out of an upstairs window. Why does everyone have a gun? I didn't realize there were so many people prepared for a zombie invasion.

The gun fires and hits one of the newly recruited zombies in the chest. The zombie crumples to the ground. I still can't get over the fact that zombies can die without having their brains destroyed. It's just not right. I push myself up against the side of the house so the man with the gun won't be able to see me. The other zombies in my group follow my lead.

Another shot is fired, but the gunman can't seem to get a good angle on us. He fires again, but the bullet hits the side of the house. My leader gestures for me and the other three zombies to join their group in front. I shake my head. I think I'll stay back here where there are fewer bullets flying at my head. The leader gives me a severe look. I reluctantly come out of my safe corner, and the three other zombies follow me to the front of the house.

The gunman sees us rounding the corner and takes out the zombie directly to my right. That was close. I look at my fallen comrade and realize that it's one of the zombies from my original trio. I stumble for a moment as I'm overtaken by a deeply hollow feeling in my stomach. I suppose this is how a leader feels when one of their pack members is killed.

I look at my leader to see if she is feeling any pain or grief about her pack member's demise, but she is focused on climbing through the window. She's probably good at compartmentalizing her feelings. Or maybe she just doesn't have a soul.

Another bullet flies past my head, but this one doesn't hit anyone. My leader is the first one to climb in the window. She has a little trouble getting in, but she makes it. She pushes a chair in front of the window so it's easier for the rest of us to get in the house.

The gunman isn't at the upstairs window anymore. He must know that we're in the house. I am the last one to climb in the window, and once I'm inside, I see one of the new pack members moving up the stairs. I am surprised that the leader isn't going up first.

Then I realize her strategy when the gunman bursts from his room and starts shooting at the zombies as they ascend the stairs. The first zombie gets shot in the stomach, and my leader takes this opportunity to climb the stairs under the cover of the other zombie from my original trio. Her shield is shot when she is only a few yards away from the gunman, and that hollow feeling overtakes me again, as my last original pack member falls to the floor. The gunman aims his rifle at my leader's head, but she pushes the barrel out of the way at the last second. The bullet hits the ceiling, and my leader lunges at the man's throat and sinks her teeth into his neck. He falls to the ground, and the rest of the pack closes in on the man. There are only five of us left, so there is more than enough meat to go around.

I am about to dig into my dinner when my leader gestures for me to investigate the room the man came out of earlier. I guess I'll have to wait a little longer before I can enjoy my meal.

I cautiously walk into the master bedroom, but I don't see anyone else in here. I am about to turn and leave when I hear a muffled whimper come from the far side of the room. I creep over to the closet and swing the door open.

One woman, two children, cowering in the corner, tear-stained cheeks, fearful eyes, cowering in the corner.

I can't kill them. There is plenty of meat in the hallway, so I'll just leave these poor souls alone. I am about to close the door when the woman lunges at me with a shovel. I grab the other end of her weapon before she can hit me. My leader looks up from her meal in the hallway. I see her smile as she comes to help me kill the woman. I think my leader has figured out that I'm unable to murder people. She probably sent me in here as a test. It looks like I failed.

The leader wraps her arms around the woman's neck and sinks her teeth in. Another zombie in the hallway sees what's happening and comes to get some of the fresh meat. As my leader is tearing into the woman, I creep back over to the closet and shut the door. I'm hoping nobody notices the children in the closet because I can't kill kids. I just can't.

I will, however, take a bite out of the woman lying on the floor because her screams have finally ceased. It's much easier to enjoy a meal when there isn't anyone shrieking in your ear. After we eat every morsel of the man and woman, the zombies start moving toward the stairs. Just when I think the kids are safe, the little boy bursts from the closet wielding a high-heeled shoe. He starts beating the leader with the heel, and she looks amused.

My leader reaches for the boy, but I block her. We have eaten enough for today. We don't need to kill these kids. My leader looks at me like I've gone crazy.

Lady, you have no idea.

She shoves me out of the way, and I stumble backward. I can't catch myself, and I end up falling to the floor. My leader gestures for two zombies to hold me down. They put all their weight on me, and I fruitlessly struggle to push them off me.

I hear the little boy scream, and I look away. I can't watch these monsters kill kids. I hear the little girl shriek as she is pulled from the closet. How can they murder children? I know these zombies were human before they were infected. Didn't they have kids? I start to realize that these zombies might not be as compassionate as I am. I can't stand to be a part of this group anymore.

The zombies holding me down are distracted by all the tender, fresh meat. It probably tastes like veal to them. I shove the zombies off of me, and I stumble out of the house and into the night. I expect the leader to chase after me, but she never comes. I guess I'm not worth the trouble.

Chapter 30

I am enjoying my newfound solitude. Sometimes it's better to be on your own. No one from my old pack has come after me, and I finally feel safe. I wander around for a few days, but I don't see any humans. I come across a squirrel, but those things are hard to catch. I eventually give up on hunting the squirrel when I realize that I'm unable to climb trees.

I'm feeling nauseous, and I can barely stand, so I decide to sit for a while. Sitting doesn't make me feel any better, but I don't have the strength to get up. I sit still until I hear footsteps coming up behind me. They don't sound like zombie footsteps, but I can't imagine why a human would be wandering through the woods alone.

I hide behind a tree as the footsteps approach. I can smell human flesh, but there's something different about it. It's mixed with another smell. Once the creature gets closer, I realize that it's an infected human. I see a large bite mark on her forearm and know that she'll be a zombie soon. Perfect! That's exactly what I need.

The infected woman is about to pass my hiding spot. She steps past my tree without noticing me. I move away from my hiding spot and am about to grab her, when a twig snaps under my foot. She spins around and screams at the sight of me. I try to snatch her, but she leaps away from me. I chase her for about ten yards, and just when I think I'm about to catch her, she jumps onto a low branch of a tree and quickly climbs away from me. That's OK. I can wait. She'll have to come down eventually.

Oh, I get it. She's just waiting up there until she turns into a zombie. That seems terribly selfish. I'm down here starving, and she's wasting all that meat. The least she can do is spare an appendage so I can have a snack.

I hear several more sets of footsteps behind me. I don't have to turn around to know they're zombie footsteps. I glance behind me anyway to see what I'm dealing with. There are four zombies coming toward me, and I'm relieved that I have never seen any of them before. I dread the thought of running into my former leader. I don't want to find out what she would do to me for deserting the pack.

The four zombies join me and start circling the tree. We're all looking up at the slowly decaying meat. I quickly figure out which one is the leader of the pack. She is trying to climb the tree, and I feel better when I see that the leader isn't able to either. I'm glad it's not just me. I loved climbing trees when I was a kid, so I'm annoyed that I'm unable to do it as a zombie.

The other zombies try climbing the tree, but none of them are successful. I consider leaving; it's clear that we're not going to get the meat sitting in the tree. I'm about to walk away when the leader of the new pack approaches me. She looks around and then gestures at me. *Yes*, I nod. *I am alone.* She sweeps her arm, pointing at each of her pack members and then at me, inviting me to become a part of her pack. I'm hesitant to join them, because of what happened with my last pack, but I really don't have any other options. I haven't eaten in days. So out of desperation, I nod to the leader, accepting the offer to join her pack.

She brings her face close to mine. It takes me a second to realize that she wants me to touch her cheek. I quickly poke at her face, and then she moves back around to the other side of the tree.

* * *

The infected woman has been up in the tree for hours. We're still standing below her, waiting for her to fall. She's holding on for her life, but she must be getting tired. I wonder if she can hold on until she turns. She smells worse as the hours go by, and I wish we could move on and try to find some other meat. I prefer meat that's fresh and within reach.

I keep glancing at the leader to see if she's showing any signs of defeat, but she just keeps circling the tree. I'm getting bored, and the meat in the tree doesn't even smell good anymore. I look up and see the woman shivering, and I think she's about to turn. Good, I'm getting tired of waiting.

The woman falls from the tree and lands directly on top of one of my pack mates. I want to laugh, but my laughing capabilities seem to have vanished along with my ability to speak. The leader rolls the newly infected zombie off of her pack member then helps him get up. The injured zombie is a bit unsteady on his feet, but it looks like he'll survive.

The new zombie woman is struggling to her feet, trying to get away. She probably doesn't realize that she's a zombie now. I'll bet she thinks we're still a threat. Well, we certainly don't want to bite her now. Zombie flesh seems so unappetizing.

The leader follows the new zombie woman and backs her up against a tree. The new zombie puts her hands up to defend herself. She definitely doesn't realize that she's a zombie now. The leader holds up her hands to show the woman that she doesn't want to hurt her. She is signaling for the new zombie to join our group.

The new zombie hesitates for a moment. Eventually, she realizes that she's one of us and follows the leader over to the pack. I guess that means she's part of our group now. I nod to the new zombie, welcoming her. I'm still a little annoyed that she didn't share her meat with us while she had the chance, but I can't really blame her.

The leader starts to walk away, and the rest of us follow. There are now six of us in the pack, so I imagine we should be able to hunt fairly easily. We walk until we come upon a dirt road, which we follow for what seems like miles, but we don't come across any humans. We run into two other zombie packs, but we just pass them without acknowledging their presence. I'm so tired, and my hunger is making me miserable. We better find some food soon or I'm not going to make it. I'm so hungry that I would eat that dog, and I would probably eat those kids I tried to save. It's awful how your morals disappear when you're hungry.

We shuffle along the road for a while until we come across a small, red farmhouse. There is a broken fence around a falling-down barn. The farm animals must have already been eaten by another pack.

The farmhouse has obviously been invaded, and all signs of life are gone, but the leader gestures for us to follow her into the house. We walk into the foyer and see furniture flipped over and doors falling off their hinges. We follow our leader upstairs and see nothing but upended furniture. We're about to go back downstairs when I notice an attic entrance directly above us.

I tap the leader on the shoulder and point at the attic. She looks up and grins. The attic is at least ten feet off the ground, so my leader finds a chair and climbs on top. She tugs on the cord that opens the attic door.

The door swings open and a massive dresser hurtles out of the attic and onto our leader. The other zombies and I pull the dresser off her, but it's too late. Her body is completely crushed. The other four zombies stare at me.

I didn't do it!

I know going into the attic was my idea, but I didn't mean to kill her. One of the zombies touches the leader's mangled face. Then he comes up to me. I assume he's going to try to hit me or challenge me. I flinch as he touches my cheek and moves away. Not good. The other three zombies do the same. Then they look at me for instructions.

Chapter 31

My first order of business as the new leader is to find some food. Obviously, there are people in the attic, or they wouldn't have put that dresser in front of the door. I don't hear anything up in the attic, but there must be someone up there.

I want to send one of the other pack members up to investigate, but these zombies are accustomed to their leader taking all the risks. It didn't turn out too well for her, but I decide to be brave and go up there by myself. I climb onto another chair and hoist myself up. I have a little trouble at first, because I'm still weak from hunger, but I'm finally able to pull myself into the attic.

I don't see anyone right away, but I can definitely smell human meat. I know someone is up here. The attic is dim and filled with cardboard boxes and plastic containers, which I assume are filled with knickknacks accumulated over the years. There is a massive trunk in the middle of the room, so I shuffle over to it and swing open the lid. There's nothing inside but musty, moth-eaten clothing. The humans must be in here somewhere. I look behind me and see two figures sitting against the wall in the far corner of the attic. I creep over to them, even though it's obvious they are already dead. They don't smell infected, but I can't be sure.

I inspect the woman and don't see any bite marks or bullet holes. She must have starved to death. There is a little boy propped up next to her, and he also has no visible wounds. I have no idea if this meat is safe to eat. I assume it's all right. I take a small bite from the woman's arm. It's not fresh, but it tastes OK. I drag the woman's body to the attic door and pass it to my pack members below. I go back to get the boy and hand his body to the others before I climb down.

My pack hasn't started eating yet. They are looking at the dead bodies and then back at me. They're probably wondering if it's safe to eat. It's better than nothing. I shrug and dig into the rotten meat, and the others follow my lead. It's definitely not fresh, but at least it'll give us enough strength to hunt.

I eat the woman's leg and then decide that I've had enough. The other zombies stop eating right when I stop. There is plenty left over, but I think we're all done with the rancid meat. My pack looks at me for directions. I get up and walk down the stairs, and they follow me out the door. It's getting dark again. We should find somewhere to stay for the night because I don't want to be around this creepy, rotten-smelling farmhouse anymore.

My stomach feels funny. I'm not nauseous anymore, but something is definitely wrong. I look back at the other zombies, and two of them are clutching their stomachs. I guess eating that rotten meat was a bad idea. I didn't know that zombies could get food poisoning. This is why I shouldn't be a leader.

I stumble back into the woods and find a clear area to sit down, feeling so sick that I can barely move. The other zombies don't look too good either. They're even more pale than usual. Even though I poisoned them, they don't seem to be mad at me.

I close my eyes and try to cope with the pain. I know I won't be able to sleep, but I try to let my thoughts take me to another place. I haven't felt this guilty in a long time. Not only did I poison myself, I poisoned my whole pack. I'm a pretty lousy leader.

As I'm clutching my stomach, trying to find a comfortable sitting position, I hear footsteps in the distance. I signal for my pack to be quiet, even though they haven't made a sound since we got here. As the footsteps approach, I hear two voices speaking in gibberish. I get up and hide behind a tree, peering out to see if the humans are a potential threat. One of the men comes into view with an AK-47 in his hands.

I signal for my pack to get up and hide behind a stand of oak trees nearby. They move as quickly as their poisoned bodies will allow and are able to conceal themselves before the hunters notice them. I can smell the humans, and they're only a few yards away. They pass our hiding place and continue walking in the other direction.

I wonder where those hunters came from and where they're going. I want to find out, so I decide to follow the hunters at a safe distance. Maybe there are more humans in that direction. My pack shuffles through the trees about thirty yards behind the hunters until a little town comes into view. That looks promising. I notice that there is a makeshift chain-link fence surrounding the town. There must be some humans in there, so my pack and I make our way toward the town.

I hear a vehicle drive past us, and I signal for my pack to duck behind a nearby group of trees. I creep out from my hiding spot to get a better view and see a small car drive up to the edge of town and stop in front of a gate. Someone with a gun walks over to the car, signaling for the people in the vehicle to come out. The driver gets out of the car, and then someone else steps out of the passenger side. Both of them start to remove their clothes, showing their skin to the people with guns. They must be checking for bite marks. Then it hits me that this town is a safe zone. Jackpot! I need to figure out a way to infiltrate the town. Then we'll be able to eat for weeks.

* * *

I sit up all night, forming a plan. To make this work, we'll need close to one hundred zombies. I don't know if we'll be able to get that many packs to cooperate, but I have to make the effort.

I feel much better once the sun comes up and the poison from the rotten meat has worn off. My pack and I head back into the woods, knowing that we'll need to be careful around this area, because those two hunters with AK-47s might come back. I assume they're trying to clear out the woods around the safe zone.

The first pack of zombies that we come across has only four members. I approach the leader and point in the direction of the safe zone. The leader nods, signaling that she is aware of the town. I raise my eyebrows in a question: what are you doing about it? The leader shrugs; she knows they can't take over the town by themselves. I gesture at her, indicating that we should join forces.

She lunges at me with a fierce look in her eyes, misunderstanding my intentions. I raise my hands, trying to convey that I don't want to challenge her. I gesture to show her that I want us to work together. She turns away from me for a moment, considering my offer, and then she nods at me.

The nine of us troll the woods for more packs. Throughout the day, we come across four more packs, and three of them agree to join us. The one pack that refused our offer had recently eaten, so they didn't feel desperate enough to join us. The other three packs, however, were getting hungry.

By the end of the day, we have thirty-four zombies in our super pack. If we can triple our numbers in the next couple of days, then we'll be ready to execute my plan. After resting for the night, our new zombie pack moves through the woods, searching for recruits. We come across a few zombies who aren't affiliated with a pack, and they are happy to join us. The stragglers are easy to enlist. They're hungry and desperate, so it doesn't take much to convince them to join our group.

We run into two more packs that have no interest in joining us, but we're able to recruit four other packs in addition to the stragglers. Our numbers have swelled to sixty-one. By the end of the day tomorrow, I hope to have enough zombies to carry out my plan.

I instruct my newly expanded pack to rest for the evening. We're going to have a long day tomorrow, followed by a long night. I don't usually like to hunt at night, because it's risky to be out in the dark. But what we're doing tomorrow is going to be dangerous anyway, and I think the darkness will work in our favor.

I get up at dawn, and the other zombies follow my lead. I can't quite believe I'm the leader of this massive pack. I split the pack into three groups to spread out and enlist more zombies. We have already recruited most of the packs in the area, so we'll have to go further into the woods to find more. My group runs into a large pack of sixteen zombies. The leader is enormous, and I'm hesitant to approach him.

Bloody zombie, huge arms, heading in my direction, no shirt, bloodshot eyes, heading in my direction.

The huge zombie stands in front of me and crosses his arms, challenging me to a death match. I have twenty zombies in my group, and it appears that he wants to absorb my pack into his. I shake my head and point in the direction of the town. He nods. He is well aware of the town, and it looks like he has the same idea, wanting to take over the town for himself.

He takes a step toward me, and I take a step back. I really don't want to fight this zombie. I won't last thirty seconds, but I can't back down. I take a deep breath and step up to accept the huge zombie's challenge just as a shot is fired into our group. I've never been so happy to hear a gunshot. Everyone panics, and the huge zombie signals for his pack to follow him deeper into the woods. I gesture for my pack to follow me in the other direction. I want to get as far away from that huge zombie as possible.

My pack follows me back toward the safe zone. I veer to the left, so we are traveling parallel to the town. I don't want to take my pack too close to the guarded area during the day. That would be suicide. The sound of the gunshots is fading, and, finally, I think we're safe. The hunters must be following the other pack. I wonder how the other two groups of my super pack are doing right now. I hope they don't run into the hunters.

I feel awful that I wasn't able to enlist any zombies today. We'll probably have to do more recruiting tomorrow. The longer we wait, the longer I put my pack in danger. Those hunters aren't going away, and I feel like we're sitting ducks out here just waiting to be shot.

As night falls, one of my two groups comes back to join us. They were able to recruit ten more zombies. So if the other group didn't lose any zombies today, we will have a total of seventy-one. That number is a bit low, but it might be the best we can do.

The third part of my pack still has not returned. I wonder if the hunters got them; or maybe the huge zombie challenged the head of that group and absorbed the rest of my zombies into his pack. Either way, I'm not going to be able to carry out my plan if the last third of my pack is missing.

I signal for everyone to sit down. Just when I have decided that we won't be taking over the town tonight, I hear footsteps in the woods. I get to my feet and signal for my pack to get back up. I know they're getting annoyed with my mixed signals, but I want them to be ready if we have to flee.

As the footsteps get closer, I see that there are about forty zombies shuffling in our direction. The zombie in charge of the third part of my pack approaches with her hands in the air, proud of her accomplishment. I don't quite believe what I'm seeing. It looks like she was able to recruit the remaining zombies from the huge zombie leader's pack as well as a few others.

I'm impressed with her recruiting skills. I wouldn't be able to carry out my plan without this zombie, so I decide to make her my second-in-command. I quickly do the math in my head; we now have a total of one hundred and two zombies. It's finally time to execute my plan. I don't want to wait another day, because I'm sure those hunters will be back.

I stand in front of the massive zombie pack and reveal my plan. Then I divide my pack into three groups and assign them each a task. Once everyone knows what to do, we make our way toward the town. I keep picturing one of my favorite scenes from *Land of the Dead*, when a horde of zombies infiltrates a city of survivors. This is going to be just as exciting!

Chapter 32

After observing the town for the past two nights, I have noticed the front gate is heavily armed, but the sides of the town are not nearly as protected. There are a few guards who monitor the fence on the sides of the town, but we should be able to get past them without too much trouble.

My group of forty-five zombies makes our way to the right side of the town while the other group of forty-five goes around to the left. On my signal, the remaining twelve zombies will walk right up to the front gate. It's a suicide mission for them, but I don't know if they realize it.

My group is in position near the right side of the fence, so I signal for the small group to start their death march toward the front gate. My group hides in the field outside the fence and will stay here until the twelve zombies are spotted. After an agonizing two minutes, the guards finally notice the twelve kamikaze zombies approaching the front gate, and they start shooting into the small group. I watch the guards from our side of the fence make their way to the front gate to help take out the twelve zombies. Now is our chance to charge the fence.

I signal for my group to follow me toward the ten-foot-high chain-link fence. There is razor wire along the top, but we're not going over the fence. My plan is to go under. Lucky for us, this makeshift fence looks like it was put up haphazardly, and it shouldn't be terribly difficult for us to get under.

I notice one lone guard standing on the other side of the fence in front of us. She's a slight woman with black hair tied in a bun. She can't be more than twenty-five years old. She spots us and starts yelling something in gibberish into the radio on her shoulder. She is probably calling for backup, but it's too late for her. Soon they'll be calling for backup on the left side of the fence as well.

The guard shoots into my group of zombies, but there's no way she can take us all down. We reach the fence and, with extreme effort, are able to pull up the bottom to make enough room for one zombie at a time to crawl under. The guard shoots at each zombie that makes it under the fence, but she runs out of ammunition after killing only five zombies. I am expecting her to flee, but she stays to fight. She takes the butt of her gun and starts hitting zombies on the head as they come up on her side of the fence. Her hoped-for backup does not come to help.

Finally, one zombie dodges the guard's blow and sinks his teeth into her shoulder. She lets out a scream, and I crawl under the fence to help the other zombie finish off the guard quickly. I feel a little bad for her as I rip into her flesh. She was brave, but not very smart. As more zombies crawl under the fence, they fall to their knees so they can enjoy the fresh meat. I gesture at them to get back up because we have more work to do. There is plenty more meat to be had, but we need to get rid of the ones with guns first. Then we can enjoy our feast.

None of the guard's meat is wasted. As the remaining thirty-seven zombies in my group pass her body, they each take a bite. Everyone is starving, but we have to stay focused. Eight of the zombies in my group were killed during the break-in, and I don't want to lose any more. We make our way to the front entrance so we can kill the remaining guards. The zombies on the left side are supposed to be doing the same.

I hear shots fired as we approach the front gate, and it looks like the zombies from the left side are already there. The guards all have their attention turned toward the others. My group needs to stay quiet so the guards don't realize we're sneaking up behind them. We are within five yards of the guards before one of them notices my group and starts firing at us. A bullet comes within inches of my head, and the zombie next to me gets shot in the stomach. I have lost so many zombies in the past five minutes that I have to ignore the hollow feeling in my stomach so I can focus on my task.

There are only seven guards remaining. We have them surrounded, and I lunge at the one closest to me. Our numbers allow us to quickly kill all of the guards, and we are able to enjoy our first feast. I don't want this meat to sit for too long, because I know what happens to dead bodies when they don't get eaten right away. We probably have a little time before the townspeople band together and try to attack us. We'll be ready for them, but now, we eat.

As I'm greedily slurping the meat, I do a quick head-count of the remaining zombies. There are seventy-two of us left. It takes less than ten minutes for us to finish every morsel of the guards' flesh. I signal for my pack to get up so we can execute the rest of my plan to invade the entire town before the sun rises. I am assuming the residents are all awake, because not even the deepest sleeper could have slept through all that gunfire.

My pack and I make our way to the center of town, and I divide the zombies into four groups. Each group is assigned to walk to the edge of town to dispose of anyone who tries to attack us. It's important that we get rid of the heroes right away. Later, we can go after the hiders.

My group starts moving toward the left side of town. A muscular man with graying hair bursts from his home with a club in his right hand. He is able to bash one zombie in the head before three others latch onto him. He screams, but falls silent within seconds. I'm sure the zombies are full, but they still take huge chunks out of the man.

We continue down the road, and two people emerge from a small house. The woman has a frying pan, and the man is wielding a rolling pin. Idiots. We surround the couple and tear them apart in less than thirty seconds. We don't finish their meat either. I hate to waste it, but we need to make sure we kill all the brave ones. Then we can relax.

We get to the edge of town, and no one else comes after us. I am sure the humans are watching, and they know they can't defeat this many zombies. We drag the bodies of the man and woman back to the center of town. I know they will be rancid if they sit out for too long, but we can enjoy them for breakfast. They should still be good tomorrow, just like day-old bagels. Thinking about bagels makes me gag. I need to stop comparing delicious human meat to the food from my former life.

I have given up any hope of returning to my human self. I know it's not going to happen. I'm actually enjoying my zombie existence. It was a little rough in the beginning, but I have finally found my place.

There are sixty-eight zombies remaining, and they are all looking at me expectantly. I signal at them to relax. We have fought enough for one night. I gesture for them to sit down in the center of town. I don't think anyone else will be coming after us tonight.

Chapter 33

We have been in the town for two days, and people have finally stopped coming out of their homes to attack us. They know they've been defeated. A few people try to shoot at us from their upstairs windows, so we break down their doors and dispose of them quickly. There are still plenty of humans, but they are locked up in their homes. We don't want to go after the hiders just yet. We need to wait until we get hungry again. For now, we have plenty of meat to go around. The brave ones are delicious.

I feel much stronger now that I have been eating a steady diet for two days. I actually feel stable on my feet, and my movements are more agile. The whole pack looks stronger too.

I have assigned a group of zombies to circle the perimeter to make sure the humans don't try to escape. We want to keep our food alive and inside the town for as long as possible. One of my zombies on perimeter duty comes up to me and gestures for me to follow him. I signal for two more zombies to come with us. I don't know what's up, but I want some protection just in case there is any trouble.

We get to the right side of the fence and see a group of five zombies standing outside. The leader of the small pack wants to join our group. Of course he does. We did all the hard work, and now he wants to reap the benefits. I look at the leader and the other four zombies in his group. That's when I notice the sixth member of the pack.

Tiny zombie, frail body, looking up at me, no shoes, sad eyes, looking up at me.

I have never seen a child zombie before. He looks tired and hungry, so I know that I can't turn this pack away. I gesture for the leader and his pack to join us. The leader looks extremely grateful. He touches my cheek as he crosses over to my side of the fence, and the rest of the zombies do the same. When the child zombie approaches, I start to lean down, but the leader picks up the child and holds him up to my face. The child throws his arms around my neck to embrace me. I am touched. It feels good to help this pack. I haven't done anything charitable in the past few days, and this gesture feels pretty damn good. I shuffle back to the center of town with the new pack members a few steps behind me.

When we arrive in the middle of town, my second-in-command approaches me with her hands on her hips. She doesn't look happy with me, and I'll bet she wants to know why we're taking in a new pack. I point at the child zombie, and she cringes when she sees him. Young zombies are rare because children hardly ever get bitten and get away alive. They don't have the strength or speed to evade attacking zombies, so they are usually devoured before they have time to turn.

My second-in-command nods at me, but she gives me a stern look. I know that we can't let in any more zombies from the outside. We worked too hard to allow other packs to infiltrate our town.

I signal to my entire pack to pay attention. The original zombies are not happy to see the newcomers. They're probably concerned that I've gone soft, and they don't want me to let in every zombie that comes by. I hoist the child zombie up on my shoulder, and a low moan comes from the crowd. I assume most of them have never seen a child zombie before. I point at the small zombie and gesture that this is the reason I let the group in. My pack gapes at the tiny zombie in wonder. I signal at them, letting everyone know that I won't let in anyone else.

* * *

The next two days pass without incident. No more zombie packs try to gain access to our town, which surprises me. I just assumed there would be a flood of zombies trying to get in. No more human survivors have emerged from their homes, so we are going to start breaking down doors. I send zombies into homes in small groups.

I follow one group to a house on the edge of town. We have seen people looking out the window, and we suspect they are trying to escape. I instruct five zombies to start working on getting the door open, and it doesn't take long to break it down. Once we are in the house, we go directly upstairs because that's usually the humans' favorite place to hide. I think, psychologically, they want to be as far away from us as possible.

There are four closed doors off the upstairs hallway. I turn to my left and can smell them in the room down the hall. I gesture for the five zombies to break open the door, which takes them a few minutes, but they're finally able to bust into the room. I hear screams coming from the corner of the room, and I enter just in time to see the zombies rip apart two women. I hate to hear people scream, because it reminds me that I'm a monster. I almost forget that I'm a zombie until I hear those screams.

Once the shrieking stops, I join in the feast. There are two bodies and six zombies. That should be plenty of meat to satisfy all of us. I am happily munching on a leg when my second-in-command bursts into the room. She gestures for me to follow her. She looks scared. I have never seen my second-in-command look frightened, so I know that we have a serious problem.

I follow her out of the house, past the center of town, and I gesture for the rest of my pack to follow me because I sense that there could be trouble ahead. There is a group of about twenty zombies standing outside the fence. It's a large pack, but we can take them down. I am feeling confident until I spot their leader. I almost turn and run. She is the most terrifying zombie I have ever seen. She points directly at me, challenging me. My original zombie leader wants to fight me to the death.

I don't want to look like a coward, so I accept her challenge. At least I'll go down fighting with a little dignity. I don't understand why only leaders have to fight to the death instead of entire packs. I would win for sure if my whole pack could fight along with me. Actually, now that I'm in charge, I get to make the rules. I wave my arms, signaling for my zombies to attack the others, and my entire pack descends on the intruders.

The other pack is caught completely off guard, and they are barely able to put up a fight. My former leader tries to punch me, but I block her and latch onto her arm. One of my pack members grabs her other arm and watches me as I snap my former leader's elbow in the wrong direction. My pack member follows my lead, and, with some difficulty, snaps her other elbow. My former leader looks shocked, but she's not done with me. She lunges at me, arms useless at her sides. I shove her away, and she stumbles for a moment but doesn't fall down. She dives at me again, but this time I grab her head and twist until her neck breaks.

I toss her body aside and join in the rest of the fight. My zombie pack is much stronger than the intruders, because we have been eating for days. My former leader's pack is weak, and we make short work of killing the trespassers. I can't help but be proud of my pack.

Just as I start congratulating myself on my newfound leadership abilities, a gunshot rings out and one of my pack members falls to the ground. I turn around and see a human army followed by two tanks, closing in fast. It's an ambush.

I signal for my pack to scatter and run. Several guns fire into the crowd. I see zombies fall all around me. My pack is being slaughtered, and I am unable to help them.

I quickly stumble down a side street to a back entrance. I turn around to check if the military is following me, and I only see three zombies from my pack trying to keep up with me. I make it to the fence at the far end of town, when a soldier spots us. She begins to fire into our small group. One of my zombies gets shot in the back and falls to the ground.

I bend down to work on prying up the fence so we have enough room to get through. Another one of my zombies is shot in the arm. I am able to move the fence enough so I can slide under. I grab the hand of the last zombie in my group to pull her under the fence. I get her out, and I'm about to turn away from the town when I get shot in the gut. The pain is blinding. I fall to the ground and clutch my stomach. I look at my wound and see that I've been hit by a dart. I pull out the dart and feel a foreign substance coursing through my veins. It burns my insides, and it feels a lot like the fluids that were injected into me back at the lab. As the poison works its way through my body, I writhe in pain until I go limp and pass out.

Chapter 34

I wake up in a dark room, freezing. I try to pull my blanket up to my chin, but I realize there is nothing covering me. I try to reach over the side of my bed to grab my blanket, but I find that I am unable to roll to my side. There is a thick, tight strap over my rib cage and another strap across my thighs. My arms are free, but I can't move anything else. I try to reach for the light on my bedside table, but the table is gone. What the hell? My eyes begin to adjust to the darkness, and I see that I'm wearing a hospital gown and slippers. I look around and see rows of beds with people strapped to them.

"Hello?" I croak. My voice isn't working properly. I feel like I haven't spoken in weeks. "Is anybody awake?" I ask.

The woman in the bed next to me speaks, "Do you know where we are?"

"I have no idea," I say.

I try to remember how I got here, but my memory is fuzzy. I remember waking up and going to work. Jason was late, so I waited for him. Then I...zombies! How could I forget? The country is overrun with zombies. I have to get the people out of here before the zombies get them.

"Excuse me," I say, loud enough for everyone to hear me. "I don't want anyone to panic, but we need to get out of here. We are all in danger."

A gasp comes from the woman in the bed next to me.

"That's enough," says a man who strides into the room and walks right up to my bed.

Tall man, broad shoulders, glaring at me, white coat, dark eyes, glaring at me.

"Where are we?" I ask the man. He has graying hair and a square chin. His deep voice makes him seem threatening, but I won't let him intimidate me.

"Somewhere safe," the man responds. "You're going to be fine. Do you feel like you have completely recovered?"

"Recovered from what?"

"Most people don't remember, and we find that it's better if we don't remind them."

"Look, you need to get these people out of here. The country has been invaded by zombies, and it's not safe for us to be strapped down like this."

"Don't you worry about the zombies," the doctor says the last word with a chuckle in his voice.

"Don't you dare tell me zombies aren't real. I saw them with my own eyes this time."

"Calm down," the doctor says to me. "There was an issue with a medication that caused zombie-like behavior, but the problem is being fixed."

"Can you please be more specific?" I say.

"We found a cure for the side effects, and we are working on distributing the cure to everyone who has experienced these zombie-like symptoms."

I have a sudden flash of Taylor as a zombie. I remember being bitten and then taken to a laboratory. All the memories are coming back to me: the packs, the leaders, zombie fight club, and human flesh. I have a vivid flashback of eating human meat. I gag and try to roll to my side, but the straps prevent me from rolling over. I turn my head to the side and vomit.

The doctor puts his hand on my head. "Are you feeling feverish?" he asks.

"I remember everything," I say as I wipe my mouth.

The doctor raises his eyebrows. "Are you claiming to remember events that occurred after you exhibited zombie-like behavior?"

"Why do you keep referring to it as 'zombie-like' behavior?"

"That is the language we have been told to use."

"Well, I was a zombie, and I remember everything."

"That's not possible. After a person is infected, blood flow to the brain is severely restricted. You would not have been able to retain any memories of the events that occurred after you were affected by the zombie-like symptoms."

"Well, I remember everything."

"What do you remember?" the woman next to me asks.

"I killed a ton of people," I say to her.

"That's enough," the doctor says.

"Did I kill anybody?" the woman asks the doctor.

The doctor doesn't say anything, so I answer for him. "Probably. I'm sure every zombie killed at least a few people."

The woman looks like she's about to cry.

"Don't feel bad," I say. "That's just what zombies do."

"Was I a zombie, too?" the man in the bed on my other side asks. I look up and see that most of the people in the room are awake and looking at the doctor for answers.

"Can you please unstrap us?" I ask.

"Not just yet," the doctor says. "We need to be sure the infection is completely out of your systems before we let you all out," he says to the room.

"What infection?" someone asks.

"Everyone in this room either took a blood disorder medication, or, more likely, came into contact with someone who had taken this medication," the doctor says. "The infection is transmitted through saliva or blood, and it causes the brain to become muddled due to lack of blood flow. Your bodies were still functioning, but your brains were sort of temporarily rewired, so you will not have any memories of the events that occurred while you were under the influence of this infection."

"What if you do have memories of said events?" I ask.

"Please save all questions until the end," he says. "Now, because the side effects of this medication caused erratic and sometimes dangerous behavior, we have to keep all of you strapped down until we are sure the infection is out of your systems."

"But I remember everything I did while I was a zombie," I say.

The doctor raises his voice so the whole room can hear. "Some of you may think that you remember what occurred while you were infected, but I assure you that it would not be possible for you to retain those memories. The lack of blood flow to your brains would not allow you to remember anything that happened. Now, if you claim to remember anything, please raise your hand."

I look around the room, and I don't see a single hand go up. The man next to me speaks up. "The last thing I remember is that my wife got really sick, and then she bit me. How do I find out if my wife is OK?" The man looks at the doctor for an answer.

"I am sure all of you are concerned about your loved ones, but we need to keep everyone here until we are sure the infection is completely eradicated. We don't want anyone wandering around outside while there are still infected people who could spread the disease. We can't let this disaster start over again. Now, I must be going, but someone will come by soon to bring you food."

The doctor strides out of the room before I have a chance to ask any more questions. I can't believe I was an actual zombie. I rack my brain for memories of the time I spent as a zombie. I remember surrounding a farmhouse with two other zombies, and I recall joining another pack with a terrifying leader. Then I remember breaking that leader's neck. The safe zone! My memories from the town come rushing back. I can't believe I actually formed a zombie army and took over a whole town. I was getting really good at being a zombie.

A woman wearing a white lab coat, white pants, and white sneakers slowly pushes a cart into the room. Her hair is in a tight bun, and her unsmiling face makes her look hostile. She carelessly places a small tray on each person's stomach. How are we supposed to eat if we can't sit up?

"Excuse me," I say to the woman. "Can you please undo our straps so we can eat?"

"I'm not permitted to do that," she responds as she places a tray on my stomach.

I look at the contents of the tray. There are two pieces of toast and dried scrambled eggs on a small plate. No fork. I haven't eaten real food in a long time, and I wonder if I'll be able to keep it down. I reach for the toast and take a small bite. It tastes OK. I try to remember what human meat tastes like. I remember it was ecstasy to eat human flesh, but I can't recall exactly what it tasted like. That's probably for the best.

The woman with the cart is making her way around the far side of the room. She doesn't look happy to be here, and I wonder if her family was killed too. I think about Casey and the boys. I can't recall how long ago I left them in the fallout shelter, but I have to make sure they're OK.

I wait for the woman to leave the room. Then, with some difficulty, I put my tray on the floor. I try to slide out of the straps, but they're way too tight for me to wiggle out of. I'll need to think of a way out of here. I pass the day trying to form a plan, but nothing comes to mind. They can't keep us here forever, so I'll just have to wait until they let us out.

Sometime in the afternoon, the same woman in white comes back in the room and gives each of us another tray of food. There is a piece of unidentifiable brown meat smothered in a yellow, gelatinous substance. I don't risk eating the mystery meat, so I just eat a hard, stale roll and put the rest on the floor.

At some point during the evening, I drift off to sleep. I wake up to a pitch-black room. I have no idea what time it is, but I assume it's early morning. The sun eventually comes up, and the doctor comes back into the room and tells everyone that we're being let out today. Hallelujah! Now I'll get to check on Casey and the boys. The doctor says that everyone's blood will have to be tested before we can be unstrapped.

Another man comes in and starts taking blood from the people at the opposite end of the room. This is going to take a while. The man slowly makes his way toward my bed, and it's finally my turn to get my blood drawn. I watch as my blood flows from my arm, and I'm relieved to see that it's no longer as thick as pudding. Once the man is done taking everyone's blood, he says he'll be back with the results so he can let everyone out. It seems like an eternity before the man comes back to the room. When he finally returns, the doctor comes with him to give us the test results.

Chapter 35

"Good news," the doctor says. "All of you are clear, so we can let you out."

The man who took our blood earlier starts unstrapping everyone in my row, and the woman in white is letting out the people in the other row. It's finally my turn, and the man smiles at me as he undoes my straps.

"Thanks," I say to him. "I can finally go home."

The doctor overhears our conversation and strides over. "We can't let anyone out of the facility until the infection is completely eradicated. We'll have to keep all of you here until we're sure it's safe outside. We're just going to move all of you to the other side of the facility for now. You'll be more comfortable over there."

"No way," I say. "You can't make me stay here. I'm going home."

"We're keeping you here for your own safety. There are still infected people roaming around outside, and we need to make sure the infection doesn't spread further."

"Can people become zombies again if they were previously infected and then cured?" I ask.

"Yes, it's possible to get infected again, which is why you need to stay here. Now, if you'll excuse me, I have to attend to other matters."

The doctor strides away, and I end up following the crowd out of the room. The man who took our blood is explaining to everyone why it's important for us to stay in the facility until the infection is eliminated. Well, that's not going to happen. I'm leaving this place today, and they can't stop me.

I search for exits while we're given a tour of the facility. There are plenty of doors that lead outside, but they are all guarded. We pass a huge window, and I see a twenty-foot-high chain-link fence surrounding the facility. Where the hell are we? I still haven't gotten a straight answer from anyone.

We are taken to a common area and told to wait there until we are assigned sleeping arrangements. There is another large group of people in the common area. I sidle up to an elderly woman and ask her how long she has been here.

"About two weeks, I think," she says.

"Do they ever let you go outside?"

"Sometimes they let us out in the yard in the afternoon."

"Have they already let you out today?"

"Not yet. Looks like rain."

I glance out the large window in the common area, and my heart sinks when I see massive storm clouds covering the sky. I cross my fingers, hoping that it doesn't rain. I really want to get out of here today, so I approach one of the guards in the corner of the room to find out what's going on.

"Excuse me, guard? I'd like to be let outside for a little while."

"I'm not a guard. I'm a welcome specialist, and my name is Jamie," the man says.

"Hi, Jamie. I was hoping that I could get some fresh air. I have been strapped down for a long time, and I'd like to take a walk outside."

"Unfortunately, I can only permit people to be outside from 3:00 to 3:30."

"What time is it?" I ask.

"It's only 1:45. If it rains, which looks likely, I won't be able to let you out at all today."

"I don't mind walking in the rain," I say.

"I know, but those are the rules," Jamie says.

"I see." I stare out the window, willing it not to rain while I wait for 3:00 to roll around.

I feel restless, so I walk aimlessly around the room to pass the time. My heart sinks further when I hear the first clap of thunder. It starts pouring rain, and I turn to look at Jamie. He shrugs, and mouths "Sorry." The rain continues, and I walk back over to Jamie and ask him what time it is.

"3:08," he says. "Sorry, there won't be any outside time today."

"Is there any way you can let me out later when it stops raining? I really need to get outside."

"Are you trying to break out too?" he asks.

"Yeah," I admit.

"You're not the only one. A lot of people want to leave to check on their loved ones. You got family out there?"

"My sister and nephews are stuck in a fallout shelter, and I have to make sure they're OK."

"If they're in a fallout shelter, they should be safe."

"They probably don't have any food left, and there's no one else who can help them. Also, my mom is stuck in Florida, and I'll need to save her too."

"The government is doing a pretty good job of rescuing people. The best thing you can do for the country is stay here until everyone is cured."

"I know, but my family is all I have left. I can't stand not being with them."

Jamie nervously glances around. "Look, I can help you, but you can't tell anyone else about it."

"I won't. I promise!" I say.

"Meet me in this room after the sun goes down. I'll help you get out of here."

"You got it. Thanks for helping me," I say.

"Don't worry about it," he says. "I lost my wife and my two little girls, so I'm happy to help someone who still has a family."

A man walks up to Jamie and tells him to report to the doctor. Jamie winks at me as he walks away, and the other man takes the recently vacated seat. I slink away from the man and sit down next to the woman I spoke to earlier.

"So, uh, how did you become a zombie?" I ask.

"Oh, I don't think we were zombies. We were just infected with a disease that made us act aggressively." She smiles and then says, "But I don't really remember much about being infected."

"That's too bad. Maybe the memories will come back to you eventually."

"I hope not. I don't want to remember. Someone told me that the infection makes you murder people. If I killed anyone, I don't want to know about it."

"Hmmm, I suppose you're right. I lost count of how many people I killed."

"You remember what you did while you were infected?"

"Yeah."

"You should probably tell the doctor."

"I did, but he didn't believe me."

"You shouldn't worry about it, dear. It's all over now," she says before turning away from me. I don't think she believes me either. That's fine; I don't care if anyone believes me. I know what I know. I get up and walk over to the bookshelf in the corner of the room. There are about twenty-five books on the shelf, and there's not much of a selection. I quickly scan the titles, but I don't see any zombie books. I pick up a tattered copy of *Catcher in the Rye*. I've already read it several times, but I won't mind revisiting my favorite fictional character from a non-zombie book.

I sit on the floor in the corner of the room and start reading, but I'm not really paying much attention to the words on the yellowing pages. I keep glancing out the window as the afternoon passes slowly. I'm almost halfway done with the book when I hear a voice from the other side of the room.

"OK, everyone, I'm going to take you to the cafeteria for dinner, and then I'll show you to your rooms," the welcome specialist says. Everyone starts moving toward the door, but I stay where I am. Jamie should be here soon, and I can't miss him. Mr. Welcome Specialist comes up to me when he notices that I'm not following the group to the cafeteria.

"Don't you want to join everyone for dinner?" he asks.

"I'm not really hungry."

"Well, I can't have you stay in here by yourself."

I'm about to ask why, but Jamie walks in and rescues me, "That's OK, Ross, I'll be in here for my next shift, so I can watch this one," he says, pointing to me.

"Suit yourself," Ross says as he follows the others to the cafeteria.

"Thanks for coming," I say to Jamie.

"No problem. We'll have to be careful because Ross might remember you and come looking for you, so we need to get you out of here quickly."

"I'm ready to go now," I say.

"Great, follow me." Jamie leads me down a dark hallway.

Chapter 36

We arrive at a door with no windows, which Jamie unlocks with a passkey. The door opens into a dark stairwell.

"Follow me, and try not to make any noise," Jamie whispers. I follow him as quietly as possible down a small metal staircase. I can't see a thing, so I have to concentrate on not falling. I stumble on the bottom step, but Jamie is able to catch me before I fall.

"Easy there," he says. We arrive at a door with no windows. "This door leads directly outside. You won't have any protection once you're on the other side. There is no fence around the area, so once you're outside, try to find cover."

"Got it," I say.

"Here," he says, handing me a Swiss Army knife. "You'll need this to protect yourself."

"Thanks for everything," I say. "Hey, are we still in Maryland?"

"Oh, yeah, we're in Frederick."

Damn. That's about thirty miles from Taylor's house.

"You wouldn't happen to have a vehicle, would you?"

"No, sorry. I never leave the facility. I have no reason to leave," he says sadly.

I put my hand on his shoulder. "Thanks again."

"Here," he says. He takes off his black button-down sweater and hands it to me. "It's probably cold out there."

I smile at him and slip on the sweater over my hospital gown. Jamie holds his passkey up to the lock, and the door opens. I slowly step outside and turn back to thank Jamie one last time, but he has already closed the door. I look out into the night, and I can barely see a thing. I'll need to find shelter, but I want to get as far away from here as possible just in case they come looking for me.

I walk out into the cold night with Jamie's Swiss Army knife in my hand. I wrap the sweater around me tightly, because this hospital gown isn't doing much to keep me warm. I know I need to head south, but I don't know which direction that is. I follow a dirt road away from the facility, hoping to run into a street sign or anything that would give me a clue as to where I am. I walk for about a mile until I hear a rustling sound behind me. I turn around and see three figures in the shadows coming toward me. I don't care if they're zombies or people from the facility; whoever they are, I need to get away from them. I turn and sprint in the opposite direction. I'm usually a fast runner, but these slippers are making it difficult to run.

I turn around to check if the figures are gaining on me, but I've put plenty of distance between us. I assume they're zombies, because they aren't moving very quickly. I slow my awkward sprint to a run and continue jogging until I can't see the three zombies anymore. I finally arrive at a two-lane road. I don't recognize the name of the street, but I follow the sign that points to I-270 South. I can follow I-270 all the way to the I-495 split, and then I'll know exactly how to get to Taylor's house.

* * *

I don't have a watch, but I think I've been walking for at least an hour by the time I reach I-270. I feel like I'm far enough away from the facility that I can stop for the night. I walk onto a ramp that leads to the interstate. Just as I suspected, it's packed with abandoned cars. I come across an SUV with the driver's door wide open. All the windows are intact, so it should be a safe place to sleep for the night. I pull my tired body into the front seat and make sure all the doors are locked, and then I climb into the back.

I lie down and shut my eyes, waiting for sleep to take me away. I finally fall into a restless sleep. I dream that I find Casey and the boys safely in the shelter, but in my dream I'm still a zombie. I try to stop myself, but I can't help tearing into their flesh and devouring every scrap of meat until they're nothing but bones. I wake up screaming, covered in sweat. The sun is shining directly in my eyes, but I catch a glimpse of two zombies circling the SUV.

I take out my Swiss Army knife and pull out the corkscrew, scissors, and knife blade. I shift to the left side of the back seat and pound on the window, drawing the two zombies over to that side of the car. Once they are on the left side, I lunge to the opposite side of the back seat and fling open the door. I jump out and start sprinting south on I-270.

I turn back and see the two zombies shuffling after me, but they're so slow that I'm not worried about them catching up to me. I still continue to sprint as long as I can, weaving around the cars sitting on the freeway. This road is a graveyard, with rotting zombie corpses and bones littering the pavement. I try not to look at the mangled bodies as I make my way through the mess.

Once I'm sure that I've lost the two zombies from the SUV, I begin walking in the emergency lane. I walk for the rest of the morning and into the afternoon, until I come to a sign that indicates the I-495 split is only eight miles away. My feet are killing me, and these slippers are really slowing me down, but I should make it to Taylor's house before dark. I finally get to the I-495 split, and it's even worse than I-270. There are smashed-up cars and an overturned tractor-trailer blocking my path. Everywhere I look, there are skeletons and zombie corpses. I keep scanning the woods on either side of the road as I make my way through the wreckage.

As I'm cautiously moving around the abandoned cars, I hear a rustling sound coming from the woods on my right. I stop walking and peer into the trees to find a massive pack of zombies moving toward me. There must be at least twenty of them, but I don't stop to count. I hop over the median and dash toward the woods on the opposite side.

I arrive at the tree line and immediately realize my mistake. There is another pack of zombies coming toward me from the other direction. Clever buggers. They must have been following me for a long time, planning their attack.

I should have known. At least I know that zombies can't climb trees. None of the trees nearby have low branches, so I start to slowly climb the closest tree with a narrow enough trunk that I can wrap my arms around.

I clumsily make my way up the tree, but I keep losing my footing because of my annoying slippers. I'm about five feet off the ground when I realize that this isn't going to work. I hang on to the narrow trunk with my left hand and reach down with my right hand to remove my slippers. I let them fall to the ground and then I go back to climbing, which is much easier with my bare feet. I'm guessing that I have ten seconds before both packs have me completely surrounded. I really don't want to get bitten again, so I scramble up the tree as quickly as I can.

By the time the zombies reach my tree, I am about ten feet off the ground, barely out of their reach. I continue shimmying up the tree until the zombies are at least twenty feet below me. I have no idea what to do now. I know that zombies are persistent, and they could be down there for days.

I continue to climb until my arms are too sore to pull me up any further. I look down; I must be thirty feet off the ground. I wonder how long I can hold on. Fortunately, I run into some luck when I hear a gunshot ring out from nearby, and I see one of the zombies fall to the ground. I look down at my savior and see four people firing their guns into the group of zombies.

"Don't worry; we'll have these things taken care of in a minute. You can start climbing down," a woman's voice says from below. I slowly start moving down the tree as the last two zombies are shot with darts.

I jump the last few feet out of the tree and land on a zombie. Sorry, dude. I look up to see who saved me.

Four women, black uniforms, pointing guns at me, green helmets, tired eyes, pointing guns at me.

"Were you bitten?" the woman in front asks me. She has long, blonde hair, and a sweet face. It looks like she has had a rough few weeks, but she's still attractive. She's one of those women who don't need makeup to be beautiful.

"No, I wasn't bitten," I say. The women holster their guns. "I made it up the tree just before they got there. Thanks for coming to my rescue."

"No problem," she says. She eyes my hospital gown. "Did you come from the facility up in Frederick?"

"No," I lie.

"Really? Then why are you wearing a hospital gown?"

"I always wear hospital gowns. They're very comfortable."

"Interesting. We're from the facility in Frederick, and we found out that patients have been leaving without permission."

"Well, you should probably try to fix that problem," I say. "Listen, thanks for helping me, but I should get going."

"I insist that you come back to the facility with us," she says, pulling out a pistol and holding it by her side. She isn't pointing it at me yet, but I assume she will be in a moment.

I point behind her. "Look out! Zombies!" I scream. All four women spin away from me to find nothing behind them. By the time they turn back, I have taken off into the woods. They can shoot me if they want, but I doubt they will.

I run until my bare feet can't take it anymore. My complaining feet remind me that I've been doing way too much running today. I duck behind a bush and listen until I'm sure the four women aren't following me. They probably have more important things to worry about than chasing after one non-compliant human.

Chapter 37

Once I'm sure it is safe, I get back on the road and walk the last mile to the exit for Taylor's house. I can't be sure if another zombie pack is tracking me, but I keep scanning the woods for movement. My feet are killing me, but I only have two more miles to go.

I trudge the rest of the way to Taylor's house, and I'm relieved to see that there are no zombies on his street. I walk up to Taylor's front door and notice that it's slightly ajar. That's not good. I silently push open the door and see that the house is a complete wreck. There is blood on the walls and carpets, and the furniture is turned over and torn apart. I take a deep breath as I descend the basement stairs.

When I reach the bottom of the stairs, I see the rotting corpses of Taylor, Greg, and Veronica. They are so decomposed that I barely recognize them. I look away from their decaying bodies as I move past them. The door to the fallout shelter is still intact. I nervously approach the door and punch in 2-4-6-8. The door creaks open, and the stench hits me before I see anything. I walk into the room while my eyes adjust to the darkness.

Three bodies, pale faces, leaning against the far wall, closed eyes, filthy clothing, leaning against the far wall.

Seeing Casey's chest rise and fall sends a wave of relief through my body. She's alive, but she's not in great shape. Owen opens his eyes as I walk toward them, and Michael groans in pain.

"Casey, can you hear me? It's Jordan. Can you open your eyes for me?"

"Jordan?" Casey croaks. "Aren't you a zombie?"

"No. They found a cure. When was the last time you ate?"

"The food ran out a few days ago. I was trying to ration it, but there just wasn't enough."

"Why didn't you go up to the pantry and get the rest of the food from there?"

"I already did that. All the food in the house is gone."

"You're going to be OK now. There are still some zombies out there, but they're being turned back into humans. I'm going down to Florida to check on Mom, and I'm taking you three with me."

Casey starts to protest, but I make it clear that I'm not leaving her here. They'll be better off if they come with me. I pull Casey to her feet, and I get Owen to stand up. I pick up Michael, who seems to be in the worst shape of the three. He can barely keep his eyes open, and his skin is frighteningly pale. Before we leave the shelter, I grab a pistol and extra bullets. I tell Casey to take one too.

"Can I have a gun too?" Owen asks. I smile, glad to see that Owen is still the same.

"No, buddy, maybe you can have one in a few years."

"OK," he says, too weak to argue.

I walk to the garage, hoping that one of Taylor's cars is still there. When I open the door, I am relieved to see his

Range Rover. I grab his keys from the basket by the door. I buckle Michael into the back seat, and Owen climbs in next to him.

"I'll be right back," Casey says. "I have to grab a few things." She walks back inside, and I hear her climbing the stairs. A few minutes pass before Casey returns. She comes back down wearing a tight, pink sweater and skinny jeans. I raise my eyebrows at her.

"This is the least revealing outfit Veronica had in her closet. I grabbed some clean clothes for the boys too. We've been wearing the same clothes for months, and I couldn't stand it anymore."

"Hey, I don't blame you. I know how you feel," I say, pointing at my hospital gown.

"Oops. I should have grabbed something for you."

"Don't worry about it. I'll pick up some clothes at our next stop."

"We need to find food," Casey says as she gets into the passenger seat.

"I know where we can find some," I say. I start the car and drive in the direction of Gardner House. The streets are still littered with abandoned cars and dead bodies, but at least we don't see any zombies walking around. I pull into the parking lot of Gardner House and turn off the engine.

"I'm going to grab a few things and get some food for you guys," I say. I hand Casey the car keys. "If there's any trouble, just drive away."

"I'm not leaving you," Casey says.

"Just stay in the car, and you'll be fine. You shouldn't have any problems."

Jordan's Brains: A Zombie Evolution

I creep to the front door with my gun in my right hand. The automatic door doesn't open when I walk up to it, so I pry it open then cautiously step inside. The reception area is dark, and there is no one at the front desk. I see a huge blood stain on the carpet, but there are no other signs that zombies have been here. I move toward the door to the stairwell.

There isn't a window in the door, so I swing it open and raise my gun in case anything pops out. The stairwell is also dark, but I can see enough to walk up the stairs safely. I creep up to the third floor and slowly push open the door to the hallway. I don't see anyone in the hall, so I quietly shut the stairwell door behind me and move toward my old room. It doesn't smell like antiseptic anymore, but it's missing the rotten odor that I have gotten used to over the past few months. It's not often that one notices the absence of smells in a room.

I pass the reception desk where Cyndi used to sit, and I notice that my name is the last one written in the sign-out book. Everyone must have left before I did. Thanks a bunch, guys. I walk over to my old room and open the door, relieved to see that everything is just as I left it.

I open the closet door and verify there are no zombies hiding inside. I grab my bug-out bag and check to make sure it still contains five bottles of water, a box of peanut butter crackers, a hunting knife, and, of course, my zombie fact booklets. It's all there. I remove the booklets and toss them in the trash. I can't believe how wrong I was about zombies. I'll have to start from scratch on my next edition.

I grab a pair of jeans from my dresser, and I dig through a pile of T-shirts until I find the one I'm looking for. I smile as I pick up the shirt that Casey bought for me a few years ago. I put it on and pull on my socks and sneakers, and, right before I leave my room, I grab my Hartford Whalers hat.

I put on my backpack and walk to the stairwell. I make it down to the first floor and sneak to the back of the building toward the cafeteria to see if there's any food left. I'm surprised by the lack of carnage here. The only sign of a struggle is the bloodstain in the reception area. I guess the zombies didn't get very far into the building.

I peek in the window on the cafeteria door and am shocked to see a large group of people milling around. I try to open the door to the cafeteria, but there is something pushed up against it. I knock on the window, but no one seems to hear me. I start to pound on the door until I get someone's attention. That's when I make eye contact with Cyndi, who runs toward the door to let me in. A large man, who I recognize as one of the nurses, helps Cyndi move a table away from the door.

"Jordan!" She flings open the door. "I sent people upstairs to look for you when the infection broke out. Have you been here this whole time?"

"No, I've been out gallivanting with the zombies. I just came back to get my supplies and some food for my family."

"I should have known you'd be out there. I'm so glad you're OK. Your family is welcome to stay with us."

"We're actually going down to Florida to find my mom. Thanks for the offer, though I would appreciate any extra food you might have."

"We're running a little low," Cyndi says, "but we can spare some."

"Thanks. That will really help us out. We have two little boys with us who are practically starving."

"Do they need medical attention? We have a doctor here."

"No, they just need food and water."

"OK, let me see what I can find."

Cyndi walks toward the back of the cafeteria. I do a quick head count, and there are twenty-four people here. They seem to have done very well during the apocalypse. Cyndi returns with two pop-top cans of ravioli and a large bag of peanuts.

"Sorry I can't spare more," she says.

"This is perfect," I say. I take the food and put it in my bag. "Thanks for everything." I give Cyndi a hug before I leave the cafeteria. I hear them pushing the table back in front of the door as I walk away. I'm so glad Cyndi and the others survived.

I'm not paying attention as I walk out the front door, and I jump when I see two zombies circling the car. I pull out my gun and shoot the closest zombie in the leg. Hopefully, someone will come along to help him soon. The other zombie lurches toward me, so I panic and shoot her in the knee. Oops. That had to hurt.

"Sorry!" I say to her as I hop into the car.

"What was that about?" Casey asks.

"I didn't mean to shoot her in the knee. I just wanted to stop her."

"No, I mean, why didn't you kill them?"

"Because there's a cure. I can't kill any zombies knowing that they could be saved. That's murder," I say.

Casey just stares at me.

The zombie that I accidentally shot in the knee is writhing around on the ground, clutching her knee.

"She can get reconstructive knee surgery. She'll be fine," I say.

"Don't you think we should put her out of her misery?" Casey asks.

"No way. You wouldn't kill a person just because they were injured, would you?"

"But that's not a human. It's a zombie."

"It doesn't matter," I say. "Look at my shirt."

Casey reads the words on my shirt out loud. "Zombies are people too."

"You gave this one to me. Remember?"

"OK, Jordan. I just don't want you getting us hurt. The zombies are still dangerous, and we need to be careful."

"I know. I will be." I hand my backpack to Casey. "There isn't much food, but it should be enough to give you guys some strength."

Casey reaches into the bag and immediately opens a bottle of water. She takes a huge gulp and hands it to Michael first. Michael takes a few small sips, and then Casey gives the bottle to Owen. She hands three peanut butter crackers and a handful of peanuts to each of the boys.

I drive away from the hospital toward my mom's house. I remember the exact route I took on my last zombie drill to Florida. This is what I've been preparing for my whole life, and I'm not going to screw it up this time.

Chapter 38

I check the clock on the dashboard and see that it's 7:04 p.m. I've had an exhausting day, but I'm going to try to drive through the night. As we cross into Virginia, I see a group of three zombies shuffling along the side of the road. They turn toward our car as we drive past them, but they make no attempt to pursue us.

It's getting dark, and my eyes are feeling heavy. I glance at Casey and see that she is sound asleep, and the boys are out as well. It's incredibly hard to stay awake when everyone else in the car is sleeping. I give myself two quick slaps in the face to wake myself up.

I drive until I can't keep my eyes open anymore. It's only 9:30, and we haven't even reached Richmond. I feel weak stopping now, but I don't want to risk falling asleep at the wheel. I pull off the road into a gas station parking lot. I'll just sleep for a few hours, and then we can get going again. I make sure all the doors are locked before I lean my seat back and fall into a deep sleep.

* * *

I feel someone trying to shake me awake, but my mind is still somewhere else.

"Jordan! Wake up," I hear Casey's voice. "They're surrounding us."

I snap my eyes open and see two zombies outside my window. I look to my right and see that there are three more on Casey's side of the car. I check the back seat and am happy to see the boys still asleep. I turn the car on and slowly put it in reverse, careful not to hit any zombies.

The zombies are smart enough to move out of the way while I back up. After backing out of the parking space, I put the car in drive and slowly move past the sad, little pack. They look awfully weak and probably haven't eaten in a long time. Hopefully, they'll stay out in the open so someone can find them and shoot them with the cure.

I pull out of the gas station and speed off, watching the five zombies disappear in my rearview mirror. I check the clock and see that it's 6:22 a.m. I can't believe I slept through the night. Now I should be able to drive for the rest of the day. I check the gas gauge, which shows that the tank is a little more than halfway full. That should be enough to get us through North Carolina.

"How are you feeling?" I ask Casey.

"Much better than yesterday," she says. She takes out the box of crackers and eats two. "So did you ever find out how all of this started?"

"Yeah, it was caused by a blood disorder medication."

"What was it like being a zombie?"

"It was hard at first. But by the end, I was good at being a zombie. I formed a zombie army and infiltrated a town full of survivors."

"Are you serious?"

"Yeah."

"That's terrible. How many people did you kill?"

"You killed people?" I hear Michael's tiny voice from the back seat.

"Uh, no, I didn't kill anybody. I was a vegan zombie," I lie.

"What's a vegan zombie?" Owen asks.

I wonder how long they've been awake. "Vegan zombies survive on, um, leaves and berries and stuff."

"So you didn't kill and eat anybody like Dad did?" Owen asks.

"I told you, Owen, that wasn't really your Dad," Casey says. "He was infected, and he couldn't control what he did."

"Whatever," Owen says.

How do you explain to a child that his dad murdered his mom because his brain was infected? That's not an easy conversation to have.

"Hey, buddy," I look at Owen in the rearview mirror while I speak to him. "There were a lot of people who were infected with this disease, and it caused them to do terrible things to their loved ones. But you can't…"

"Look out!" Casey screams. I hit the brakes right before smashing into a lone zombie. I watch in horror as the zombie flies backward and slams into the pavement. I put the car in park and open the door.

"What are you doing?" Casey asks.

"I have to make sure he's OK."

"It's a zombie; it'll be fine. Didn't you say they only die if you destroy their brains?"

"Oh, yeah, turns out that's not true. The zombies are still alive, so you don't have to destroy their brains to kill them."

"What?" Casey says incredulously.

"I know. It's ridiculous, right?"

"So these things aren't dead?"

"Nope," I say. "Their brains are jumbled, but they're still alive."

"So, if they're not dead, then I guess they're not actual zombies."

"Why does everyone keep saying that? Of course they're zombies," I say. I carefully drive around the crushed zombie, and I don't think he'll be getting up. Rest in peace, jaywalker.

"Are you guys OK?" I ask the boys.

"I'm hungry," Michael says. Casey gives them each three crackers.

"Don't worry, guys. We should get to Grandma's house by tomorrow morning at the latest."

"Is Grandma OK?" Michael asks.

"Yes, Grandma is fine," Casey says.

I hope Casey is right about that. I drive in silence until we cross into North Carolina. I know we are close to where I met Sarah, the car thief, at that campground. I wonder if she survived the zombie invasion.

"Do you want me to drive?" Casey asks.

"No, I can drive the whole way. You just relax," I say.

"I'm capable of driving."

"Yeah, but I've done this before, and I know exactly where to go. Besides, you need to regain your strength," I say. Casey concedes and lets me drive in peace.

Chapter 39

We make it into South Carolina without having any more run-ins with zombies. I see a few shuffling along the side of the road, but they don't bother us. I haven't seen any humans yet. We come across the occasional abandoned car, but the back roads are mostly clear.

I start to get nervous when I realize the gas tank is almost empty. I want to fill up before it hits the red E. Casey keeps falling asleep and waking up, but the boys have been sleeping for most of the morning. I nudge Casey and ask her to hand me my backpack.

"What's going on?" she asks.

"We just need some gas."

"Are there any gas stations open?"

"I doubt it. I'm going to find a car that I can siphon some gas from." I pull over next to an abandoned sedan with the driver's door open. I take the small, clear hose from my backpack and grab a gas can from the trunk of Taylor's car. Casey starts to follow me out of the car.

"What are you doing?" I ask.

"I want to help."

"You can help by staying in the car."

"You need someone to keep a lookout for zombies."

"Fine," I say, "but stay close to the car." I walk over to the driver's side of the abandoned car and reach inside to pop the door to the gas tank. I walk to the side of the car and open the cap to the tank and stick the hose in. I place the gas can on the ground and start to suck on the hose. I look up and see Casey scanning the road behind me. As I see the gas start to rise from the tank, I stick my end of the hose into the can. The gas flows from the car for a few minutes then trickles to a stop. There isn't as much gas as I'd hoped; I'm guessing it's about three gallons. That'll have to do for now. I stand up and remove the hose from the tank.

"Jordan! Behind you!" Casey screams. I draw my gun and spin around to find nothing behind me.

"What the hell?" I turn back around to find Casey laughing at me.

"Gotcha," she says.

"That's not funny," I say. "Haven't you heard of the story about the woman who cried zombie?"

"Aw, don't be mad. I was just joking."

"Hilarious," I say. I'm annoyed with Casey, but I can't help smiling. I'm glad to see that she's back to her old, silly self. I fill our tank with the commandeered gas, and then I hop back in the driver's seat and turn on the car. The gas tank shows that it's a third of the way full. That will have to do for now. I start driving again, and, before I know it, we're in Georgia. Casey leans over and taps the gas gauge.

"I know," I say. "I've been looking for more cars to siphon gas from, but I haven't seen any."

"Yeah, I've been looking too. What if we try another road?"

"I don't want to get lost. This is the only way I know. I think I see a car up ahead." I pull up next to a large, blue SUV, and I hope they have enough gas in their car to get us to Jacksonville. I get out of my car and walk around to the trunk to get the hose and gas can. Casey opens her door.

"Nope," I say, "you stay in the car."

"Come on, Jordan, I was just kidding last time. I won't do it again. I promise."

"Fine," I say. "Can you check to see if the driver's door of the car is unlocked?"

Casey gets out to inspect the blue SUV. "The driver's door is locked. So is the back door," she says.

I walk around to the other side of the car, and those doors are locked too. The small door to the gas tank is one of those fancy ones that you have to open by pushing a button on the inside of the car. I look around and spot a rock on the side of the road. I pick up the rock, which feels like it weighs about five pounds, and I walk over to the left side of the car.

"Stand back," I say to Casey. I hurl the rock at the window on the driver's door, but the glass only cracks a little. I pick up the rock again and throw it at the cracked window, which shatters easily this time.

"What are you doing?" Owen asks. I spin around and see Owen standing next to the car.

"Get back in the car!" I yell at him.

"No. I'm tired of being in the car," he whines.

"Casey, can you deal with him, please?" I say. I unlock the driver's door, trying to avoid the broken glass. I reach in to pop the door of the gas tank. I see Casey ushering Owen back in the car and telling him to stay put. I stick the hose in the gas tank and kneel down to draw out the gas. There is residue left in the hose, and the taste of gasoline fills my mouth, which makes my eyes water. I hate that. When the gas finally starts flowing from the tank, I put my end of the hose into the gas can. There seems to be a lot more gas in this tank. I stand up next to Casey and scan the area.

"What's that?" Casey asks as she points into the distance.

"That's a zombie, but he's by himself. We have a few minutes before he reaches us."

"Do you think we have enough gas? Should we go?"

"Not yet. I want to get as much gas as possible from this car," I say. "Let's just stay here for another minute. He's not going to get to us by then." The zombie is stumbling in our direction, and it's obvious we're his intended meal. I turn away from the zombie and check behind us to make sure no one is coming at us from the other direction. I'm relieved to see no one there.

I turn back around and see the lone zombie is about thirty yards away from us, and I'm satisfied that we have enough gas. I pull the hose out of the tank and grab the gas can.

"Are you going to fill our tank now?" Casey asks.

"No. Let's drive down the road for a mile so we can fill up while we aren't being hunted by a zombie."

"Good idea," she says.

I put the gas can and hose in the trunk and hop in the front seat. I look in the rearview mirror and see the zombie is still twenty yards away. I start the car and drive down the road for a few minutes.

"Is this a good spot to fill up?" Casey asks. She nervously looks at the gas gauge that is now on E.

"Sure," I say. I stop the car in the middle of the road and walk around to the trunk to retrieve the gas can. I start to fill the tank while looking back in the direction from which we came. I turn in the other direction and see no signs of activity. Once all of the gas has been transferred from the can to my tank, I put the can back in the trunk and walk around to the front of the car. That's when I see a pack of eight zombies closing in on me. I sprint the few feet to the driver's door and scramble into the car.

"Where did they come from?" Casey asks.

"The woods, I would imagine. They love lurking in the trees." I start the car and speed off just as the first zombie reaches my door, and I'm careful not to hit any of them. "I didn't realize there were so many left. I guess it'll be a while before all the zombies are cured."

"I suppose," Casey says. "How long before we get to Mom's house? It's getting dark."

"I think it'll be a little more than two hours," I say. "We have plenty of gas now, so it should be smooth sailing."

When we pass Savannah, I think about stopping by Doris's house to check on her, but I don't know if she would want to see me again. When I went to return her car, I saw the troubled look on her face as Casey explained to her that I have psychotic tendencies. I hope Doris knew that I was just trying to help her.

Chapter 40

At the Florida state line, someone has put up a makeshift roadblock using a tractor-trailer to cover the entire width of the four-lane road. I can't even get around it by driving on the grass, because there are obstructions on either side of the trailer. It looks like someone doesn't want anybody passing through. It's dark outside, so I'm leery about getting out of the car to investigate.

"Why would someone block the entire road like that?" Casey asks.

"I don't know. Let's see if someone comes out." We wait for thirty seconds, but we don't see any movement on the other side of the roadblock. "I guess I should go check it out," I say.

"Are you sure? Shouldn't we wait until morning?" Casey says.

"That's a good idea. I'd rather not walk around in the dark. Let's drive back in the other direction for a few miles so we can find a place to stay for the night. Then we'll come back when the sun is up," I say.

"That sounds like a good plan," Casey says. "I don't want to sleep right outside this roadblock. Something seems off about it."

I turn the car around and drive for about two miles before I pull over on the side of the road.

"This looks like a good place to stay for the night," I say. "I can't believe it's already 10:00."

"Thanks for driving all day."

"No problem."

I check on the boys in the back seat, and they're sound asleep. They have slept for most of the day. I know these past few months have been traumatic for them, and they must be exhausted.

"Good night," Casey says. I smile at her and lean my seat back.

* * *

I wake up to the sound of someone banging on the window.

"Hang on," I say. I rub my eyes and peek out the window to find four zombies circling the car. They look gaunt, and I'm assuming they haven't eaten in weeks. I turn on the car and slowly drive away from the zombies. I really don't want to hit any of them, but they won't get out of my way. They must be desperate for meat.

"Zombies!" I hear Owen scream from the back seat. Casey's eyes snap open, and she gasps.

"I know, buddy. I'm getting us out of here," I say.

"Just run them over!" Casey says.

"No, they'll move eventually," I say.

The four zombies hover around the front of the car as I inch forward. This could take a long time. I check my rearview mirror and see that it's clear behind me. I put the car in reverse and step on the gas. The car flies backward, and we leave the zombies behind.

I slam on the brakes, and then put the car in drive and start to speed toward the group of zombies. Right before I reach the pack, I jerk the wheel to the left and swerve around them.

"See. That wasn't so hard," I say. I glance at Casey and see that she's bracing her arms against the dashboard. She doesn't say anything, but I can tell that she's annoyed. We arrive back at the roadblock, and I see three men standing in front of the tractor-trailer.

Fat men, filthy clothes, holding shotguns, red faces, huge scowls, holding shotguns.

I turn off the engine and look at Casey. "Stay in the car. I'm going to go talk to those guys."

"Um, no, you're not. Look at them. I doubt they have good intentions," Casey says.

"I'm sure it's fine. I'll just ask them if they'll move a few things out of the way so we can pass."

"Absolutely not. Let's just leave and find another way to get to Florida." The three men start approaching the car. "Jordan, drive!"

"Fine!"

I turn on the car and throw it in reverse. I hear the men yelling after me, but I can't make out what they're saying. Once we're far enough away that they can't shoot us, I slam on the brakes and quickly turn the car around. I check the rearview mirror and watch the men as they fade into the distance.

"I guess we'll just have to find another route. Can you check the glove box for a map?" She opens the glove compartment and the only thing in there is a GPS.

"Why don't we try this?" Casey asks.

"I doubt there's a signal, but you can try it."

Casey plugs in the GPS. After a minute, a message pops up.

"Signal not found," Casey says.

"That's OK. We don't need it. We'll just find another way," I say.

We drive for a few miles until we see a sign for I-95.

Casey starts to say, "Why don't we just…"

"Nope."

"Jordan, why can't we just check the highway? It might not be so bad."

"I know it's going to be a mess. We shouldn't waste our time."

"We're almost there. Why don't we just try? If it's bad, we can turn back."

"I saw a visitor center a few miles back. I'll bet they have a map there," I say.

"I'm hungry," Owen says.

"Me too," Michael chimes in.

"We'll be there soon, guys," I say.

Casey pops open a can of ravioli and hands it to the boys. "Try not to make a mess," she says. Owen grabs the can and takes a handful of ravioli and then hands the can to Michael. The back seat is already covered in red sauce. Their mother would be freaking out right now, God rest her superficial soul.

I follow the signs to the visitor center and pull into the parking lot. There are two other parked cars, but no one is inside either of them. "I'll be back in a minute," I say. I grab my gun and get out of the car, closing the door quietly behind me.

I cautiously move toward the door of the large, brick building. I peek inside the window, but there's so much grime on it that I can barely see inside. I carefully push open the door, and I cringe as it lets out a loud creak. Holding my breath, I cross the threshold of the building. I'm sure if there were any zombies in here, they would have shown themselves by now. I let out my breath and cross the room to a tourist display. I quickly grab a map of Georgia and Florida and then head back toward the door.

"Freeze," a voice says from behind me. Very slowly, I turn around.

Short woman, blonde hair, pointing a gun at my head, scared eyes, trembling hands, pointing a gun at my head.

"I don't want any trouble. I just came for a map," I say. The woman doesn't take her eyes off my face. She looks like she's in her early thirties. I'm sure she was pretty once, but the apocalypse has not been kind to her. She's still pointing her gun at me, so I say, "My family is waiting for me outside. We're good people, and we're not going to hurt you." The woman studies my face. Then she lowers her gun.

"Are you from Connecticut?" she asks, pointing at my Hartford Whalers hat.

"No. I'm from Maryland. I'm just a fan of the Whalers."

"But the team doesn't exist anymore," she says.

"I know. That's why I like them."

She gives me a strange look. I'm about to tell her that I live in a psychiatric hospital, but I decide against it. Instead, I say, "Do you need any help?"

"We just need some gas. We were running low and didn't want to get stranded on the road, so we holed up here. We heard that there's a cure, so we figured it would be safe to come out soon."

"There is a cure, and it's safer than it was before, but there are still a lot of zombies out there. Where were you headed?"

"Gainesville, Florida. My husband is there."

"I can help you get some gas, if you want to get back on the road. Do you have more people with you?"

"Yes," she says, but she seems hesitant to say any more.

"OK, well, I can probably find you enough gas to get you to Gainesville."

"Thanks. That would be great," she says. "I'll be back in a moment." She disappears behind a closed door and comes back out a minute later followed by two little girls. They can't be more than five years old. They're both wearing grimy floral shirts and jeans. "This is April," the woman says, pointing to the older one. "And this is Ginger."

I smile at the girls. "Hi, I'm going to help get you out of here." They both hide behind the woman. "Follow me," I say.

I walk out into the sunshine and signal for Casey to pop the trunk. I grab the gas can and hose from the back. "I'm just going to give these people a little gas," I say.

"Who are those kids?" Michael asks.

"They're just some people we're helping out," I say.

"Can I play with them?" Michael asks.

"No, I want you to stay in the car." Owen opens his door and hops out. Brat. "OK, Michael, you can get out and play too, but stay close to the car."

"You would be an awful parent," Casey says as she gets out of the car.

"I know." I watch the boys walk up to the girls, who seem shy, but happy to see other kids.

"Which car is yours?" I ask the woman.

"The blue one."

I walk over to the other car and am happy to see it's an older model, so I won't have to break any windows to get the door to the gas tank open. I stick the hose into the gas tank and go about my usual siphoning routine. Once I have gotten as much gas as possible out of the tank, I bring the full can over to the woman's car so I can add it to her tank.

"Thanks again," she says.

"No problem. I'm happy to help."

"What's your name?"

"Jordan. You?"

"Linda."

"That's my mom's name," I say with a smile. "We're going down to Jacksonville to make sure she's OK."

"I'm sure she's fine," Linda says.

"Zombie!" Casey screams.

"Everyone, get in the car!" I yell.

I run toward the boys, but before I can get to them, I hear a gunshot. I walk around the car and see the zombie lying on the ground, and then I turn to see Linda pointing her gun in the direction of the fallen zombie.

"I'm impressed," Casey says.

"I've gotten good at killing those things," Linda says.

It makes me cringe to hear people call them "things." Not too long ago, I was one of those things. "You know, there is a cure," I say, "so it would be a good idea to spare as many zombies as possible, since they're still technically living, breathing human beings."

Linda just stares at me.

"Well, we should probably get out of here," I say. "Linda, good luck getting to Gainesville."

"Thanks for the gas," she says.

I usher the boys back into the car. I open the map and check out our options.

"It looks like US 23 is our best bet," I say to Casey.

"You're the boss."

I wait for Linda to pull out to make sure she gets on the road safely. I follow her until I get to US 23, then I wave at their car and turn onto the road that will lead us to Mom.

CHAPTER 41

As I pull onto US 23, I see that it's far worse than I expected, but the road is passable. I spend the first few miles swerving around abandoned cars, but at least it's not packed like the highways. I begin to get anxious when we arrive at the exit for Jacksonville. My shaking hands wipe the sweat from my forehead.

"I'm sure she's fine," Casey says to me.

We arrive at the entrance to Mom's community, and I realize I haven't mentally prepared myself for this. I have always assumed she was OK, but now I'll finally have an answer. I see my mom's car sitting in her driveway, and I pull up next to her house and turn off the car. I put my head on the steering wheel, telling myself that she's OK.

"Are you all right?" Casey asks.

"Fine," I say. "You stay here with the boys. I'll just make sure it's clear inside."

"No. We'll all go," Casey says. I don't argue. I just grab my gun and slide out of the car. I walk up to the front door with Casey and the boys right behind me. I try to turn the doorknob, but it's locked. I pick up the fake rock by the front door and remove the key. I let everyone into the house and then close the door behind me.

"Mom?" I call. There's no answer.
"Mom?" Casey tries.
I hear footsteps coming up the basement stairs. Thank goodness. I rush to the top of the stairs and am greeted by an unwanted visitor.
Large zombie, pale skin, lunging at me, sunken face, bloodshot eyes, lunging at me.
Casey runs up next to me and shoots the zombie in the chest. He tumbles backward and falls down the basement stairs. I notice that the back door is wide open.
"Maybe she left," Casey says.
"I don't think so," I say. I creep into the basement and step over the dead zombie. It smells like rotten meat down here. I walk up to the door of the storage room and take the extra key from the ring above the door. I unlock the door and put my hand on the knob, but I can't bring myself to open it. Casey comes up beside me and puts her hand over mine. We both turn the knob and open the door together. The smell hits me first. My eyes adjust to the darkness, and I see a figure curled up in the corner.
Rotting body, pale skin, holding a note, eyes open, mouth agape, holding a note.
I stumble over to the corpse and fall to my knees. I cradle my mother's body to my chest, and I feel Casey wrap her arms around me. I inspect my mom's body for bite marks, but there are none.
"It's my fault," I say through my tears.
"Please don't blame yourself," Casey says, trying not to cry. I know she wants to stay strong for me, but I can tell that she's devastated too. She takes the note from Mom's hand and reads it to herself.

"What happened to Grandma?" Michael asks. I didn't even notice the boys walk into the room.

"She didn't have any food or water left," Casey says, "and she couldn't leave the room because the zombies were outside."

"The zombies," I growl.

"Jordan, are you OK?" Casey says.

"The zombies."

"Jordan, you're scaring me. Look at me."

I push Casey away as she tries to help me up. "I'll take care of it," I say.

"Take care of what?"

"I'll do it myself," I say, pacing back and forth. I grab Casey's gun from her hand and stride out of the room.

"What are you doing? Jordan, don't do anything stupid."

I take the stairs two at a time. I run out of the house and scream, "Get out here! I know you're there. Come out, you cowards!" I walk into the street and see a zombie shuffle out of the house next door. I walk right up to her and put a bullet in her brain.

"Aim for the head. That's what they all say."

"Jordan! Please, stop. You're scaring the kids," Casey says from the doorway of our mom's house.

"Get back inside!" I scream. "I'll take care of it." I see two more zombies come out from behind the neighbor's fence. "I see you," I scream. I sprint toward them and aim my gun at the closer zombie. I shoot him in the face, and then I aim at the second zombie, hitting him in the forehead.

"Zombies aren't real, they say. Zombies don't exist. Who's crazy now? Huh?" I see an elderly man looking out his window at me. "What?" I scream at him. "What are you looking at? You think I want to do this? I don't. But I have to. That's what Dad wanted."

I spin around and see that there is no one on the street. I calmly walk over to my car and pull the keys from my pocket. I get in and start the engine. Then I slam on the gas and speed off down the street. I have no destination, just a purpose. Rage courses through my veins, and I can feel it infecting my body.

I spot a pack of zombies up ahead. I put my foot all the way down on the gas and slam into the four of them. I love the way it feels as my car crashes into the zombies, and they are crushed under the wheels. I don't check to see if they're all dead. It doesn't matter. I scan the street for more victims and see a lone zombie up ahead.

He is hobbling in the other direction, but I catch up to him quickly. I pull my car up next to him, roll down my window, and put a bullet in his brain. I enjoy watching the blood ooze from his head as he crumples to the ground.

I drive around until I spot two more zombies, and I smile as I pull up behind them. They turn when they hear me coming. I put my car in park and jump out. Then I raise my gun and shoot the first zombie in the head. I aim at the second one and pull the trigger, but nothing happens.

I don't have any extra bullets, so I lob the gun at the second zombie's head, but it only slows her down for a second. She shuffles right up to me and lunges at my face. Before she can bite me, I punch her in the throat. She stumbles backward, and I sock her directly on the nose. The zombie falls to the ground, so I take the opportunity to stomp on her chest and then kick her in the head. She tries to claw at me, but I leap out of the way. One more time, I stomp on her face, and then I grab her head and twist. The sound of her neck breaking is so satisfying, but it's not quite enough. I grab her head and slam it into the pavement until it's an unidentifiable bloody mass.

Just as quickly as the rage took over my body, it leaves me, stunned, sitting on the pavement. I stand up and notice that I'm covered in zombie blood. I check to make sure I don't have any cuts or scrapes on my skin. After I confirm that I don't have any wounds that would cause the zombie blood to infect me, I wipe my hands on my shirt and walk to my car. I calmly drive back in the direction of my mom's house.

Chapter 42

I park next to my mom's car and walk inside the house, leaving a trail of bloody footprints behind me. I trudge into the living room and find Casey sitting with the boys.

"Jordan, are you OK?"

"I'm fine."

"Did you get bitten?"

"No."

"What happened?"

"Nothing." I turn and walk upstairs.

"Jordan, you're getting blood everywhere," Casey says, following me up the stairs.

"I did what Dad wanted me to do."

"What?"

"Doesn't matter."

"You're scaring me," Casey says. "What can I do to help?"

"I just need a shower."

I turn away from her and finish climbing the stairs. I slam the bathroom door behind me and strip off my clothes. I turn on the shower and feel the water with my hand. It doesn't get hot, but I don't care. I step in and stand under the freezing water for as long as I can bear it, watching the blood wash down the drain. I feel much better when I get out of the shower. I dry myself off and look in the mirror.

"You're a murderer," I say to my reflection.

I wrap a towel around me and walk to my mother's room. I'm a lot bigger than my mother, but I rummage through her closet, trying to find something that will fit. I have a completely different body shape than my mom, but I don't have any other options. I grab a pair of black sweatpants and a large shirt with a picture of a black cat on it. I pull on the ill-fitting clothing and then glance at myself in the mirror. I look ridiculous. The pants only come down to the middle of my calf, and the cat shirt isn't doing me any favors. Oh well, it'll have to do for now.

"You OK?" Casey asks as she joins me in Mom's room.

"Never better."

"You were gone for a long time."

"I just had to take care of something."

"I see. Well, I secured the back door, so we should be OK to stay here for the night. The television and radio aren't working. I did find some food in the pantry, so that should be enough for our trip back to Maryland."

"I'm not going back," I say.

"Why? You can't stay here by yourself."

"You and the boys should stay with me. We could start a new life here."

"I don't know. I feel like we should go back home. Don't you want to go back to Gardner House?"

"No. I'm done with that place. We always wanted to move away from Maryland. I think we should stay here."

"We'll see," Casey says.

Owen walks into the room. "Can I play outside?"

"Me too?" Michael asks.

"It's not safe outside," Casey says.

"It's OK. I'm going outside anyway to dig Mom's grave. They can come with me," I say. Casey tries to protest, but I wave her off. "I'll watch them."

The boys follow me to the first floor, and I continue down the stairs into the basement. "I'll be right out," I say. I walk to the storage room and open the door. I kneel beside my mom's corpse and kiss her forehead. "I'm sorry," I say.

I lift her body and carry her up the basement stairs. I know she's heavy, but I barely feel the weight as I walk outside with her in my arms.

"Why are you carrying Grandma?" Michael asks.

"I'm going to bury her, and we're going to have a nice funeral for her this evening."

"Can I help?" Michael asks.

"Of course you can," I say. "Why don't you pick a spot for us to bury her?"

"I found this shovel in the garage," Casey says.

"Perfect, thanks."

"Over here," Michael says, pointing to a spot by the garden.

I walk over to where Michael is standing and lay Mom's body down by her future grave. I take the shovel from Casey and start digging. I dig until my hands are so sore that I can't take it anymore. I hop out of the three-foot-deep grave to take a break.

"You done?" Casey asks.

"No. I'm just resting. I want a six-foot-deep grave."

"Are you worried that the zombies will get her body if it's not deep enough?"

"Zombies don't like meat that's been dead for too long. It's poisonous to them."

"Did you hear that in one of your zombie movies?"

"No. While I was a zombie, I got poisoned by eating meat that had been dead for a long time."

"Gross," she says. "Do you remember everything about being a zombie?"

"Yeah, but I don't want to talk about it," I say.

"I understand."

I'm about to hop back in the grave when I notice a zombie coming around the left side of the house. I run right up to her and slam my shovel into her head. The zombie falls to the ground, and I hit her repeatedly until I know for sure she won't be getting up.

"I want to go inside," Michael says.

I turn around and see Casey ushering the boys inside. "I'm going to finish digging, but I'll be in soon," I say.

I walk back over to the shallow grave. Before I resume digging, I wipe the blood off the shovel. I don't want any zombie blood tarnishing my mother's grave.

It's almost dark by the time I finish digging. I go back in the house and call out to Casey and the boys. "It's time." I hear them coming down the stairs.

"Is it safe outside?" Michael asks.

"Yeah, I'll protect you," I say. They follow me out into the yard, and Casey helps me place Mom's body in the grave.

"I'll miss you, Mom," Casey says. She takes the best-looking half-withered rose from the garden and places it on Mom's stomach.

"Bye, Grandma," Owen says.

"Bye, Grandma," Michael echoes.

I kneel down next to my mom's grave. I don't even realize that I'm crying until I see my tears falling on my mom's body. "I'm sorry, Mom. For everything. I wish I wasn't such a disappointment to you. I tried to be normal. My brain just doesn't work right, and it probably never will. But I know you still loved me. And even though you were always frustrated with me, I always loved you. And I always will."

I get to my feet and grab the shovel. I hear Casey sob as I cover our mom's body with soil. I see Mom's legs disappear first, followed by her torso. I cover her face last, and then she's gone. I pack the soil down with the shovel then place a rose on her grave.

"Bye, Mom," I say. I follow Casey and the boys back into the house, and I trudge up to my mom's room so I can read the note she left. Casey gave it to me earlier, but I wasn't ready to look at it yet. I take the note from my pocket and read it to myself.

Jordan,

I know you came for me, and I'm sorry I couldn't hold on. There are too many of them outside. I just ran out of water, and the food has been gone for a while. Please don't be sad for me. I'm probably one of the only people who could find some joy in the apocalypse, knowing that you finally got to live your fantasy.

I know I always gave you a hard time about your fascination with zombies, but I was worried about you. I didn't want you to waste your life. But it makes a mother feel good to know that her child was able to find happiness, no matter how strange it might be. I have always admired you for your enthusiasm. Some people skip from hobby to hobby, never really finding what truly makes them happy. Jordan, you discovered your passion at a young age, and you stuck with it. I know it wasn't a normal pastime, but at least yours turned out to be useful.

I wish I could have held on longer. But since I have to leave you, I wanted to let you know how very proud of you I am.

Love to you, Taylor, and Casey,

Mom

Two Months Later

CHAPTER 43

I really like living in Florida, and everything is pretty much back to normal. The power is back on, and stores are re-opening. The grocery store right up the street just opened yesterday, and it's nice to be able to get gas at an actual gas station instead of siphoning it from abandoned cars.

I was watching the news this morning, and they said that the highways are finally being cleared. That doesn't matter to me though, because Casey and I decided to stay in Florida with the boys for a while. Michael and Owen will be starting school soon, and they're actually excited about it.

I haven't seen a zombie in over a month, and the people on the news claim the infection that caused people to exhibit "zombie-like" behavior has been eliminated.

"What are you doing?" Casey asks as she comes into the family room followed by Owen and Michael.

"Just watching the news," I say.

"I'm tired of the news," Casey says, taking the remote from my hand.

"Can we watch cartoons?" Michael asks.

"Let's see what's on," Casey says. She flips through the channels. "Look, Jordan, *The Walking Dead* is on. Do you want to watch it?"

"No, that's OK. We can watch something else. I think I'm over zombies."

"No way! I don't believe you," she says before switching the channel to a talk show.

"It's true. I'm done with zombies."

"So what are you going to obsess over now? Vampires?"

"Don't be ridiculous."

"I know you, Jordan. You always obsess over something. What are you going to fixate on now?"

I look at the boys and smile. Then I put my arm around Casey. "Family," I say.

"Aw, that's so sweet." Casey puts her head on my shoulder.

"Gotcha!" I say. I snatch the remote from Casey and flip back to *The Walking Dead*.

"I should have known," Casey says before punching me in the shoulder.

I smile at her and settle in to watch my zombie show. I'll never get tired of stories about walking corpses. Everyone needs an obsession to pass the time, and mine just happens to be zombies. That doesn't mean I'm crazy.

Author's Note

I have left Jordan's gender ambiguous, because I didn't want the story to be shaped by the main character's sex. Originally, I was going to reveal Jordan's gender at the end of the book, but I honestly couldn't decide if I wanted Jordan to be male or female. I'd like to think that it doesn't matter. Jordan is a lot of things: a friendly psychopath, a pleasantly naïve optimist, and a Good Samaritan. But I have left it up to the reader to decide if Jordan is a man or a woman.

I would like to thank you, dear reader, for taking the time to read my book. I hope it was enjoyable for you. I also want to thank Kenric, Mom, Dad, Scribendi, and CreateSpace for editing this novel (your feedback and support were invaluable). Linda, thank you for helping me brainstorm (you have the most wonderful brains). And, of course, I have to express my endless appreciation to Kenric, for watching countless zombie movies with me.

If you have any questions or comments, I would love to hear from you:
Twitter: http://twitter.com/JordansBrains
Website and Blog: http://jordansbrains.com
Email: jordansbrains@gmail.com

Made in the USA
Columbia, SC
15 October 2018